Obedience

Volume One

Lizzie B Brown

I0573089

Copyright © 2024 by Lizzie B Brown

All rights reserved.

No portion of this book may be reproduced in any form without written permission from the publisher or author, except as permitted by U.S. copyright law.

Cover created by GetCovers.

Contents

A Message to the Readers

I'm so happy you decided to read Obedience Volume One. Before you start, I want to be clear that Obedience is an ongoing romance serial written for Kindle Vella and Patreon. This collection is the first twenty-four episodes combined and reformatted.

Future volumes will continued to be released for readers who prefer this format.

Content Warnings

This is a story about a sexual relationship between a 40 year old college professor and his 21 year old student. The book contains adult themes that include: Domme/sub, dubcon, age gap, somewhat public sex acts.

This is not a manual on how to form a healthy Domme/sub relationship. There is a level of toxicity and immaturity on purpose because it is part of their journey and growth.

For more information regarding content warnings for Obedience or any of my other work, please visit lizziebbrown.com.

Debbie,

This wouldn't exist if you hadn't started me down this path. Everything I create is because of that little push you gave me years ago. Look at me now, writing smut about a college professor that's obsessed with his student. Thank you for your support and friendship over the years.

To all my readers who love an older man that knows his place is on his knees.

Episode 1
The End of Summer

Joshua

The white noise of random conversations hummed, almost drowning out the Beach Boys song playing on the jukebox in the dimly lit bar. It was packed tonight. The smell of sweat and seawater made an interesting combination when mixed with the whiff of perfume every time our waitress walked by our booth. You would think with it being so close to the end of summer that the crowds would have thinned out by now, but they hadn't. There were still just as many people here this Friday night as the last one and the one before that. I guess in Florida, the summer never ends.

"To the end of summer vacation," Eddie proclaimed, raising his shot glass.

"To the end of summer vacation," I replied before downing my shot. The liquid burned as it traveled down my throat, filling my belly with warmth.

This beachside bar has been our go-to spot three nights a week since Eddie dragged me away for the summer. We liked it here, despite how packed it always was, because it was only a few blocks away from our seaside rental. The short walk home had been a godsend more than a couple of times as we stumbled home, wasted.

This impromptu trip was Eddie's idea. Partying like a college student all summer didn't feel right, even if I wasn't teaching any summer classes for once. I preferred to spend my downtime being productive. Spending all day playing pickup games of beach volleyball and repeatedly failing at surfing didn't feel productive. Yet here I was and, as much as I hated to admit it, I was enjoying it. Even falling off that damn board in the ocean over and over was a breath of fresh air.

"Y'all need another shot, fellas?" The sexy, southern twang of our waitress, Daphne, cut through the noise. Her green eyes sparkled as brightly as her sunny smile as she looked down at us.

"Just a rum and Coke, Daph," I answered. I gave her a tight smile, trying my best to not seem too friendly.

Without sparing Eddie a glance, she grabbed the empty shot glasses and fluttered over to the bar. I watched with annoyance as Eddie's eyes zeroed in on her perfectly plump ass as she walked away. Daphne had curves in all the right places and it was a beautiful sight, but I would not spend my last night here making a fool of myself. Eddie had that covered already.

"Josh, you have to do something about that while we're still here. This little, self-imposed dry spell needs to end. We came here for a reason," he said, pulling his attention back to me.

Daphne had been shamelessly flirting with me since our first night here. Occasionally I would flirt back, but I had always been cautious to not lay it on too thick. Leading the poor girl on was the last thing I wanted to do. I wasn't looking for a summer fling. I wasn't looking for anything.

"That is *your* reason for bringing me here, but it isn't the reason I agreed to come. I just needed to get away," I huffed.

After Janet dumped me, I was a complete mess. We had been high school sweethearts who parted ways when we went to different colleges. The first breakup was mutual, both of us too young to make anything long-distance work. It seemed like the smart thing to do at the time. Who wants to be tied down in college?

We went our separate ways and had the stereotypical college experience with nothing to hold either of us back. Of course, we lost touch pretty quickly, both of us too consumed with our new lives. A part of me had always regretted not keeping in touch. Just because a relationship wasn't feasible didn't mean a friendship was off the table. For whatever reason, though, we let each other fade away into distant memories.

I didn't see her again until our ten-year high school reunion. Janet was standing across the room, mingling amongst the crowd of former classmates. All the memories and feelings from back then flooded me until I was drowning. Before I knew it, I was marching across the room to say hello.

The conversation flowed effortlessly. It was like we had never been apart. We danced and laughed the night away, unable to deny the spark that was still between us. When the evening ended, we promised each other that this time we would keep in touch. I had no intention of losing her again.

The build to a new relationship had been slow. We had separate lives in separate cities, neither of us wanted to throw away what we had worked so hard to achieve. We still found a way to make a friendship work.

For years, I settled for whatever time we could spare. It gave us the chance to build something more. Slowly, the casual emails turned into flirty texts. Then came the long phone calls that kept us awake half the night. The conversations always flowed so easily with Janet.

After a few years, we started alternating visits. That is when our relationship turned physical, though still not exclusive. I always waited for the next three-day weekend with excitement to see her.

When Janet's job transferred her to the big city only thirty minutes from my sleepy college town, I was over the moon. It was finally time to take the next step.

We started dating exclusively before she signed her new lease, not that I had been dating much once we reconnected. Janet was everything I needed. No one had ever made me as happy as she had. The last five years had been perfect. At least, that is what I had thought.

Janet disagreed.

"You need to move on. What better way than with a sexy brunette that has been practically presenting herself to you every night we come here?" Eddie said with a wiggle of his eyebrows, like some sort of sitcom actor.

Daphne had made her interest in me known from the very first night. I knew exactly what the little touches meant and understood the motive behind her offer to show us around town. I was grieving, not blind. My initial brush-off hadn't fazed her at all.

"Not interested," I mumbled flatly.

As if on cue, Daphne approached with my drink in hand. She made a big show of leaning over as she placed the beverage on the table, giving me a very clear view down her low-cut top. Already a few drinks in, it took me a little longer than it should have to look away. There was no missing the smug satisfaction in her smile when I finally made eye contact. I almost felt bad knowing this wasn't going anywhere.

"Anything else I can get y'all, Joshua?" There was an alluring quality to the way Daphne said my name. I felt my dick stir and scolded myself over the reaction. Nothing was going to happen.

"Not to interrupt, Daph, but I could use a drink," Eddie chimed in.

A sudden flush washed over Daphne's sun-kissed skin and her eyes widened as she realized her mistake.

"Crap! I'm so sorry, Eddie. I didn't mean to ignore you! Bourbon on the rocks?" she offered sheepishly. I couldn't help staring as she batted those long eyelashes Eddie's way.

"That's okay. I get it. Professor Salt 'n' Pepper is way more interesting than me," he teased her with his usual charm.

Daphne giggled, and I felt a flash of jealousy, something I had no right to feel. If I wanted, I could have had her in my bed long ago. By the looks she was giving me earlier, I still could.

"I'll be right back," Daphne said apologetically before rushing off. This time, I sneaked a quick peek as she walked away.

Eddie gave me a disapproving look from across the booth. My best friend since middle school had a very different view on how I should handle my newly single life. If it was up to Eddie, she would have already been in my bed, along with a string of other women. The comments about Daphne had been ramping up the closer we got to heading home. He made it very clear just how foolish he thought I was for passing up on someone like Daphne.

"No." I shook my head, prepared for yet another argument about it. If nothing else, the man was persistent.

"Is it the age thing? Ten years isn't that big of a deal. She doesn't seem to care," Eddie pushed, refusing to let it go this time.

Age wasn't the issue. Daphne's interest, despite the age difference, was a bit of an ego boost. At just the other side of forty and fresh out of a relationship, I was a little worried women might find me past my prime. The notion was probably ridiculous since I constantly had students flirt with me, but nothing shakes your confidence like a breakup. That was why I had tested the waters a few times by flirting back with Daphne. Something I now regret. A little post-breakup validation was not worth the current conversation.

"I know you think she is attractive. I've caught you leering just as much as I have."

"I don't leer," I insisted. Yes, there may have been some lingering glances, but he talked like I was some gawking creep.

"Sure, sure," Eddie waved his hand dismissively.

"It's just—" I stopped short of confessing.

The truth was Daphne would make a great girlfriend, not a rebound or a one-night stand, if the situation was different. As a fellow educator, she spent most of the year teaching at a high school a few towns over. She worked at the bar over the summers to earn some extra cash while she visited her grandparents in town. Part of why we hit it off was our shared passion for education.

Daphne deserved better, but Daphne wasn't actually the issue. I would have been just as defiant about the hot, red-headed surfing instructor or the gorgeous girl with ebony skin who ran the same route as us every morning.

"Just what, Josh? I haven't been pushy because I thought something would click once we got here. You don't have to jump into another relationship just because you jump into someone's bed," Eddie said, his brow furrowed with concern.

"The jumping into bed is the problem," I admitted. "I had been with Janet for so long, and she didn't really explain much, just that it was over."

I always assumed I was satisfying Janet. The sex was frequent, and she could never wait to rip my clothes off when we were together. But that could have been a farce. It wouldn't be the first time in history a woman faked attraction to a man. Everything could have been an elaborate ruse to keep me from knowing just how awful I was in bed.

Our breakup was pretty quick and impersonal. Janet called me on a Monday morning with three words: *we are over*. When I tried to ask for an explanation, she hung up. I made a handful of attempts to reach out in the week that followed, but she never responded. What did I do wrong?

The grip on my glass was turning my knuckles white. "What if..."

Eddie raised his hand to cut me off. "I'm gonna stop you right there. I may not know what the final nail in the coffin was, but I know for a fact your performance had nothing to do with it."

"And how would you know that? Did you and Janet have a heart to heart?" I asked, rolling my eyes. Eddie was never a fan of Janet, something he shared freely after both breakups.

"Of course not, wiseass. But Carla did." I leaned in closer as Eddie smirked, knowing he had my attention.

Carla was a coworker of Eddie's who had a little crush on him. He wouldn't admit it, but I could tell he felt the same. In her attempts to stay in Eddie's orbit, she had gotten to know Janet and me. We'd often hang out as a group, though looking back maybe it was more like double dating. Unlike Eddie, Carla seemed to get along with Janet just fine.

"Apparently, the sex is why she didn't break things off sooner. She told Carla you are like a dominating sex god or something," Eddie said, all smiles.

I leaned back, trying to process this new information. Did that make everything better or worse? On the one hand, *sex god* had a nice ring to it. However, his statement implied things had been bad for a while and I had no idea. That brought a whole new set of fears and insecurities to the table. Just how clueless was I?

"Who is a dominating sex god?" Daphne asked as she set Eddie's drink on the table. There was a glimmer of excitement as she looked between us.

Embarrassment took hold and set my body on fire. I should have been proudly strutting like a peacock, shouting from the mountaintops that I, Joshua Grant, was a sex god, but that wasn't me. It wasn't like I was a prude or anything. I just always believed there was a time and a place for such things. Now was neither. Pretending I wasn't red as a tomato, I silently took a sip of my drink.

Eddie was taking great pleasure in my discomfort. The traitor nodded in my direction. I made a mental note to remember this the next time I saw him with Carla. Let the asshole see how it feels.

"According to my ex, apparently," I grumbled. I cast my eyes down, hyperfocused on my drink. If there was a God, then I wished he would open the ground and let it swallow me.

Daphne softened her demeanor and trailed her fingers down my arm. The soft touch felt nice and inviting. The small act had my body aching for more. It had been far too long since I had experienced even the simplest acts of intimacy. Maybe I needed to just get laid, like Eddie thought.

"I've got some prep work in the back, but I'll check on you boys in a bit. Okay?" Daphne said, giving my arm a supportive squeeze.

I huffed at Eddie as she walked away, ready to surrender to his proposal. Getting laid might actually do me some good. I shouldn't be seconds away from bending Daphne over just because she squeezed my arm. God knows my hand could use the break.

"Not Daphne. We leave tomorrow and I'm afraid..." I trailed off, not sure how to convey what I was feeling. You would think teaching college level writing classes would make me a better communicator.

Even though I got dumped before the break, everything still felt raw emotionally. Maybe it was the lack of closure or the emotional void Janet left. Regardless, a hookup with someone I had already formed a connection with felt too dangerous. I didn't trust myself not to get attached. I needed to keep my walls up just a little while longer.

"Fine. A complete stranger," Eddie acquiesced as he looked around the bar. "That should be easy with it as busy as it is."

My heart picked up the pace ever so slightly. I was really going to do this. I would be lying if I said I hadn't felt the urge to fuck this whole time. Spending almost every day at the beach surrounded by half-naked women had been a constant temptation. The only thing holding me back before was the fear of rejection. I just didn't want to go through that again.

"Her," Eddie said as he pointed to a young blonde at the bar. A *very* young blonde.

Episode 2
Worship on a Bathroom Floor

Joshua

"Jesus, Eddie! She looks too young. No," I declined.

"You already said age isn't an issue. She just took a shot, so she is at least twenty-one," he said with a shrug.

"She looks like a college student. I'm a PROFESSOR!" I whisper-yelled as if she could hear us.

"At a college several states away. She isn't your student," Eddie countered. He tilted his head with raised eyebrows, silently telling me to at least consider her.

I paused for a moment to really look at her and assess the situation. The mystery girl was on the shorter side and thin, with small curves. Her blonde hair had that damp, beach wavy look girls had after a swim in the ocean. I could just make out the straps of her bathing suit peeking from the neckline of her sundress.

Her skin was barely sun-kissed. Most of the locals had a dark tan from year-round sun exposure, so she probably wasn't from around here. That thought left me with unease, but I knew realistically the chances of us being from the same town were slim. I definitely hadn't seen her around campus before.

Glancing back at Eddie, I sighed with defeat. He had the most annoying smile plastered on his smug face. I would have punched it off of him if I hadn't been secretly excited.

I tried my best to psych myself up as I walked to the target. Each step felt heavy as I closed the distance. This was no big deal. I had hit on plenty of girls when I was her age. Yeah, I was also in my twenties then, but I could still do this. Things couldn't have changed that much since I was single last.

I was still in great shape at forty, with only a small sprinkling of gray throughout my dark hair. Janet always said it made me look sexy. Okay, thinking about Janet was the last thing I needed to be doing right now. I was about to hit on a beautiful, incredibly young woman. My focus needed to be on her.

The age difference didn't worry me. Plenty of students had passed me notes with their writing assignments in the past. I had always ignored their advances because, even if I hadn't been in a committed relationship, I was their professor. But this girl wasn't my student, and I was single. There was nothing to stop me from approaching her except the crippling fear of rejection.

My palms started to sweat. The attempted internal pep talk was doing more harm than good. By the time I reached the bar, I was having serious doubts about what I was doing. Nervous, I looked back at Eddie for the last minute moral support that I desperately needed. The idiot gave me two thumbs up, not even trying to be inconspicuous. Better than nothing, I guess.

I turned my attention back to the girl, squeezing into an open spot next to her. She didn't seem to take notice of me at first, giving me a chance to get a better look at her.

Up close, she was beautiful. Soft lips curled into a small smile as she read something on the screen of her phone. Perfectly manicured nails tapped the glowing screen. Her skin had a dewy sparkle from a faint dusting of sand mixed with the salty ocean water. She must have come straight here from the beach.

"Can I help you?" she asked with a slight edge to her voice.

Crap. I had been so lost in admiring her, I didn't realize I was staring. Her baby blue eyes were peering up at me questionably. The faintest appearance of a scowl was present. Well, this wasn't getting off to the best start.

Way to go, Joshua. Just be as creepy as possible.

I took a breath to calm my nerves, filling my lungs with her intoxicating scent, a mouthwatering mix of cherries, vanilla, and the ocean. I was practically drooling for a taste.

Fuck, my cock liked that idea. It roused at the mere thought of licking her. Thank God this girl wasn't a mind reader, because she would have been horrified at all the lewd thoughts running through my mind. If everything went according to plan, I was going to explore every inch of her with my mouth.

"I was hoping to help you, actually," I said, trying to turn on the charm. Resting my arm next to her on the bar, I leaned into her space while flashing a smile. "Can I buy you a drink?"

Those blue eyes stared up at me for what felt like an eternity. Each second I waited for her answer chipped away at my confidence. The nervous feeling from before was now a knot in my stomach twisting inside as I waited for the inevitable rejection.

This was stupid. I was stupid for thinking such an attractive young woman would want me to buy her a drink let alone have sex with her. She probably had younger guys, guys her age, buying her drinks all the time. She didn't need a creepy, middle-aged man hitting on her. This was all a mistake. I braced myself for the oncoming rejection.

Just as my smile faded, it happened. She moved closer, pressing her body against mine. My breath caught when I felt her palm on my chest. Electricity radiated through my body from the contact. Her hand slid down my body at an achingly slow pace until she had my clothed cock in her hand. I stood there frozen, unable to breathe, while she coaxed me to fullness in the middle of a crowded bar. Of all the scenarios that had been playing in my head, this one took me completely by surprise.

"Instead of a drink, why don't you follow me to the bathroom?" She whispered the offer seductively in my ear. The implication was obvious: she was offering to skip straight to sex. Her lustful voice sounded like an angel desperate to fall from grace. What would it sound like when she moaned my name while on the edge of climax? I needed to find out.

Heavy with need, I tried to thrust into her hand, but my beach girl had already pulled away. I stood there for a second, dumbfounded, as I watched her walk toward the back. My gaze shamelessly lingered on the way her hips swayed as she walked.

I was lost in the haze of desire and lust this random girl left behind. All the blood was rushing south, leaving me dizzy and confused. Was this really happening right now? Was I really going to follow her?

My feet started moving on their own, my body having decided for me. I was desperate for more of her touch. Yes, I was definitely doing this. I was going to have bathroom sex with some hot stranger almost twenty years my junior. Something to cross off my nonexistent bucket list.

My heart raced as I followed her through the crowded bar and weaved around the other patrons. It took an amazing amount of patience to not plow through the throngs of people that blocked my way. My sex-addled brain was barely aware of things like manners.

The bathrooms were in the back of the bar, down a small, dark hallway. No one ever seemed to linger back there, which I found myself grateful for in the moment. There were two single stalls labeled *Dude* and *Dudette* on wood planks tacked to the lime green doors. I think it was supposed to be driftwood to go with the beach theme, but I was never very clear on the matter.

I reached the back hallway just in time to see her walk into the one labeled *Dudette*. She turned and made eye contact, effectively freezing me where I stood. Those baby blues locked on mine as she licked her lips and closed the door.

Fuck me. Please, God, fuck me.

My pace picked up as I rushed eagerly to what was waiting for me on the other side of the tacky green door. Her body was beckoning me to enter and claim her, or maybe it was just desperation after denying myself for so long. My dick was at full attention, throbbing and needy. The promises of sweet release lay just on the other side of that door.

I quickly entered the bathroom and locked the door behind me. Hopefully, no one would need to get in here until we were done.

Heaven help the poor soul that knocked. I could not be held responsible for my actions if we were interrupted.

The dimly lit bathroom, while not pristine, was drastically cleaner than the men's room. It was something I hadn't thought about until I was standing inside. As hard as I was, I doubt it would have stopped me even if it had been a disaster zone. I would have gladly fucked her next to the dumpsters out back if it meant I could be balls deep inside her in the next five minutes.

I needed to get a handle on myself before the desperation became obvious. The last thing I needed was to cockblock myself by coming on too strong. This was just sex. I have had sex plenty of times. No big deal. Except that I hadn't had sex with a twenty-something since I was twenty-something.

The object of my desire sat on the counter next to the sink with her legs spread slightly apart. She leaned back against the mirror for support, arching her chest out. I couldn't help noticing her skin was flushed and her nipples poked through the fabric of her top. The signs of her arousal were maddening in the best way. My body reacted in kind as my erection throbbed in its constraints.

I swallowed while trying to decide if I wanted to make the first move or to let her. My mind was too scrambled with lust to think straight, only seconds away from ripping our clothing off so I could feel her everywhere. I was a starving man staring at a grand feast.

The only thing holding me where I stood were those beautiful blue eyes. Her stare felt like a collar around my neck, holding me in position until I was given permission to move. I was at the mercy of this beautiful creature.

Her hungry gaze traveled down my body, stopping at the very obvious tent I was pitching. I stood a little straighter in response in an awkward attempt to show off. Inside, I was cringing at my need to impress her, but she didn't seem to mind. Her lips parted as her tongue poked out, giving them a hungry lick as I preened under her gaze.

That was all it took to break me.

I closed the distance between us and pushed between her legs. My fingers tangled in her hair, pulling her closer. Distance was the enemy.

A growl escaped me as we crashed together in a searing kiss. My tongue forced its way past her lips, devouring her like a starving man. She parted for me with little resistance, submitting to my body's demands.

I positioned my other hand on her lower back to keep her from escaping. Not that she wanted to, if the grinding and moaning were any indication. Her hands were busy exploring my body, rubbing my abs under my shirt. *Thank you, three months of keeping active on the beach.* The touch of her fingers on my bare skin sent little shocks of pleasure through me, working me into a frenzy. My blood was pumping like fire through my veins. I needed to get rid of the barriers between us and soon, or I was going to embarrass myself.

I took a step back and popped the button on my pants when she spoke.

"On your knees," her soft voice ordered.

"I'm sorry, what?" I asked, panting for breath. Her words weren't connecting.

"You'll get yours, but me first. Now be a good boy and get on your knees," she instructed. There was an edge to the command that was hidden by her gentle tone. She was serious.

I had never had a woman take charge like that before. She sat there, still gasping for breath with her kiss-swollen lips slightly parted as she watched me, waiting for me to obey. I looked down at the floor, pretending to inspect it while I stalled and tried to decide what I would do.

I was always in charge. The rush of being the one in control was something I savored during sex. It came so naturally to me. Giving up that power was foreign territory. But was I willing to risk this moment by pushing back?

With a deep breath in, I closed my eyes and dropped to my knees. The promise of tasting her sweetness was just too alluring to deny her.

"You look like you are about to pray," she giggled.

I couldn't help the small smile that crept over me. It was such an odd thing to say at the moment.

"Only fitting, since I am about to worship a goddess," I replied as I removed the bikini bottom she had been wearing under her dress.

There was a small laugh in response, but I barely registered it. The moment I saw what was waiting under that bathing suit, I was lost to the world. I trailed soft kisses up her thigh until I reached her sweet pussy. The first lick was long and slow. I wanted to tease her. I needed her to be as desperate as I was. My eyes fell shut as I savored her taste mixed with the salty ocean. My blonde goddess had been swimming.

I licked between her folds and swirled my tongue around her clit, experimenting with a few moves until I figured out how to make her moan without restraint. Once I found my groove, I was relentless. Her fingers threaded through my hair, gripping tightly as she rode my face. She was completely lost to her own pleasure, and it was the hottest thing I had ever experienced.

"Don't stop. I'm so close." She let out a strained moan. There was a wildness in her plea that made my cock ache with the need to see her come.

I growled with hunger as I slipped a single finger into her dripping wet pussy. She was so worked up that it slid right in despite how fucking tight she was. God, she would feel amazing squeezing my dick like this. My tongue continued to swirl her clit as I pumped my digit inside of her. My blonde was weeping from the pleasure I was giving her.

I curled my finger, reaching for that special spot inside her. Her climax came fast and hard. The way her body tensed around me as she let out a cry had my cock leaking in my pants. Her walls spasmed around my finger as I continued to shower her clit with attention. Her voice was becoming hoarse from all her screams of ecstasy.

I stood up once she relaxed and took in the sight of her. She was so beautiful slumped over, flushed and panting for breath. A sense of pride washed over me, knowing I was the cause.

"Condom?" she asked breathlessly, breaking the moment.

Condom? *Fuck*. I didn't have a condom. Janet and I stopped using them long ago because she was taking other precautions, and I didn't come to Florida intending to get laid. There wasn't a reason to keep a condom on me until now.

"You don't have one?" she asked, obviously noticing the panic on my face.

"No. I, um, don't. Do you?" I inquired apologetically, already knowing the answer. If she had one, then she wouldn't have asked me.

Suddenly, all the warm glow of our tryst was gone, replaced with a dark cloud of disappointment. Maybe she would take a turn on her knees? Though I didn't like the idea of making her get on the floor, even if I had just done it.

"That's fine. You can just touch yourself for me," she stated, like it was the most obvious thing in the world.

"I'm sorry?" After all that, was she suggesting I masturbate?

"No one has ever eaten me like that before. You deserve to get off, too. I want to watch you make yourself come," she said, rubbing her hand over the bulge in my pants.

I wanted to argue that if I did such a good job, then she should be the one rewarding me, but I didn't. There was a tiny voice in the back of my head pushing me to indulge her request. If I didn't think about it too hard, the voyeuristic aspect was kind of hot.

"You want to watch me stroke my thick cock for you?" I asked as I unzipped my pants. I don't know why I said it like that, but she didn't seem to mind.

"Yes," her soft voice responded.

Once free, I gave it a few tugs, smiling at how intently she watched. Once more, I felt the pull of her eyes as she watched me. Those blue eyes held a power over me I didn't understand. I needed them on me, watching me. Her gaze was the like the sun lighting my darkness and bathing me in warmth.

Suddenly, she grabbed my hand and shoved it between her thighs. I moaned as she rubbed her soaked pussy against my palm, drenching my hand. This woman was amazing.

"All lubed up," she said as she let go.

Fuck me, that was hot. Where did this vixen come from?

Using her climax as lube, I began fisting my cock while she watched. It felt awkward at first, but there was something about the way she watched that made me feel desired. Her gaze alternated between my face and my hand pumping my dick, like she couldn't decide which was more fascinating.

My pleasure was a performance for her, an offering to my young, beautiful beach goddess. Using the mirror behind her, I positioned myself in a way that seemed more flattering. I have no idea what women want to see when they ask a guy to jack off for them, but I hoped this was close.

"See what you do to me, baby?" I asked as I stroked my length from base to tip. "This is all because of you and that delicious pussy. Look how hard tasting you made me."

That devilish tongue peeked out, licking her lips as she watched a bead of pre-cum form. I bit my lip, unable to contain my hungry moan under her rapt attention. I needed more. I couldn't be this close without touching her.

"May I?" I asked, reaching for her breasts.

She nodded as she pushed her dress off her shoulders, then she slid her bikini top up. Those perfect breasts with perfect nipples were a magnet for my hand. Her skin was so soft and sticky, no doubt from her day frolicking on the beach. I could picture her running down the shore splashing in the cool ocean water.

Each breast was a perfect handful. I alternated between the two, grabbing and kneading her flesh. When I tweaked a nipple between my thumb and finger, she let out the most adorable moan. I needed to hear that sound over and over.

"Slow your thrusts," she ordered, as if she knew how close I was.

I didn't argue or question the command. At some point, I had resigned myself to the fact that she was calling the shots. My purpose in this moment was to submit to every desire she commanded of me.

Obediently, I slowed my pace to stave off my orgasm for just a little bit longer. It was a delicious torture. One that I could end at any moment if I wanted to, but I didn't. Not without her permission. My grunts strained as I forced myself to keep the slower pace. I would not disobey.

"Faster," she whispered the command, "and look at me."

I hadn't even realized my eyes had closed. I opened them in time to watch as she pulled my hand from her breasts and pressed it to her mouth. Another moan escaped me as she sucked on my thumb. The warmth of her mouth reminded me of her sweet pussy. She swirled her tongue with an eagerness that made me curse it was my thumb and not my cock.

"Baby, I'm close. I—I want to scream your name when I come," I panted out the plea.

"No." Her voice was way too seductive to be denying me.

"Please, baby," I asked again as I felt a familiar pressure building.

"No." She denied me again.

That word was pissing me off. Each denial felt like I was being unjustly punished. She had praised me earlier. Why wouldn't she tell me her name? Or even a fake name? I had done everything she asked so far.

The frustration was bubbling beneath the surface, threatening to boil over at any moment.

"Please, please. I *need* your name! I will do anything, just tell me. *Please*!" I was begging now. She had me begging. No one ever made me beg during sex.

Excitement coursed through my needy body as she leaned into me. Her lips were mere inches from my ear. I waited on the cliff of my climax for the one word to push me over. All I needed was her name.

"Come," she whispered, her final command.

And just like that, my orgasm ripped through me, drowning me in euphoria. My body shuddered as I painted my hand white with cum. I cried out a colorful series of swears since my only request had been denied. My body had betrayed me by obeying her desires over mine.

"Good boy."

I frowned as the words left her lips. She didn't notice, too busy grabbing paper towels.

"Then why won't you tell me your name?" I stood before her, pouting like a petulant child. My only request was denied.

She looked at me for a moment with a thoughtful expression on her face. Did she even have a reason, or was she lording her power over me? Why was it getting under my skin like this? I didn't really need her name. This was the only time I would ever see her.

But I wanted it. I wanted something real to hold on to on the dark, lonely nights when I recalled this moment. I wanted something that made it feel real.

"Because I don't want to and that is a good enough reason," she finally answered.

No words came out when I opened my mouth to respond. Conflicted, a part of me wanted to argue with her and make her see reason, but I also didn't want to upset her. Even though we were done and would never see each other again, I still craved her approval.

Maybe it was because I was still wounded from the breakup. There was nothing like having your entire world crash around you because the woman you loved rejected you to make you doubt your worth.

My blonde beach goddess refusing me her name hurt because it felt like another rejection, but maybe it wasn't. She let me do things to her, taste her, feel her. There were probably things at play in her life that made her refusal perfectly reasonable, and I just needed to respect her boundaries.

"You're right, my apologies," I finally conceded. Her smile made my compliance worth the hurt I still felt.

You have no idea what you have done to me, do you?

After we cleaned up, she gave me a quick peck on the lips and left me alone in the ladies' bathroom. I took another minute to collect my thoughts, still not understanding what had happened. Whatever it was, I felt happy to have experienced it.

As soon as I opened the door, my bittersweet mood turned completely sour. Daphne stood there, staring back at me. As dark as the hallway was, I could still see the tears welling in her eyes. How long had she been on the other side of the door? How much had she heard?

Rationally, I knew I had done nothing wrong. Daphne and I were not together. We never had been, and we never would be. But I had flirted back occasionally. And I never outright shut down her advances or stopped Eddie from encouraging her.

Our sweet, summertime waitress deserved better. My eyes broke away from hers in shame as the guilt poured over me. Was crushing Daphne worth my little bathroom tryst? The fucked up part was my answer. Yes, it was completely worth it.

I barely stopped to acknowledge she was there, rushing past her. The bar was still hopping, and the other patrons were blissfully unaware of what had just occurred. I weaved through the crowd of happy drunks to the booth where Eddie was still waiting for me.

"You were gone for a bit, buddy. Did you get lucky?" He smiled.

"We are leaving," I said as I pulled a hundred-dollar bill from my wallet and placed it on the table. This place was suffocating me, and I needed to get out.

"Um... is everything okay, man?" Eddie asked, concern written on his face.

"Fine. Let's just get going," I insisted.

"Ooookay," he said, finally getting with the program.

Part of me wanted to look and see if *she* was still around or if she made a hasty escape like I was planning, but it wouldn't matter either way. We had our moment, and it was over. All that was left was the memory. That would be more than enough to get me through my lonely nights for a while. It had to be.

Episode 3
Back to School Blues

Joshua

It was the first day of the fall semester. While the summer had been fun overall, I had been more than eager to get back into my routine. I needed a sense of normalcy if I ever wanted to recover from the love of my life dumping me.

Except I wasn't thinking about Janet during the quiet moments anymore. I wasn't lying awake at night dreaming of her begging to come back to me. My journal entries were no longer incomprehensible dribbles from my broken heart. While that should have been great news, signs that my broken heart was on the mend, a new agony had taken its place.

That little bathroom tryst in Florida was consuming me, and I couldn't figure out why. We didn't have sex. In fact, she technically wasn't the one to get me off. Yet, I couldn't get her or that night out of my mind.

I had given Eddie a very vague version of what happened during our flight back, only telling him she counter-propositioned me, and I gladly accepted. I was too ashamed to admit to him that a twenty-something had me masturbate while I begged for her name. Also, I was too ashamed to admit to myself how much I enjoyed it.

Every time I thought about it, about her, my cock would get hard. It wanted me to try again and succeed where I had failed. Because I *had* failed or things would have gone differently. I would have gotten her name. We would have left together to spend a night of primal fucking until dawn.

Maybe it was because I hadn't had a condom? As soon as I got home, I went to the drugstore, bought a case, and popped three in my wallet. I would never make that mistake again. The next time I would please her correctly, and she would reward me with her name and more.

At least, that is what haunted my fantasies every night. The hard truth was, I would never see my beach goddess again. That was why I needed my job and routine. If I was busy, then I wouldn't have time to think about her.

Normally, I taught four or five classes in a semester, but the administration wanted to ease me back into things after my pre-summer state. I should have been embarrassed at how much my personal life had affected my work, but at the end of the day, I was just thankful the administration was supportive. I still had a job.

Three classes may have seemed like a lighter load, but that was more than enough to keep me busy. Two of my classes were on the larger side, so there would be plenty of papers to grade. Staying busy was my current priority, at least until I worked the beach goddess fantasies out of my system.

Mondays and Wednesdays, I taught English 101 in the morning and Creative Writing after lunch. Tuesday and Thursday mornings were English 102, which left the afternoons for office hours, and Fridays were to finish grading papers and preparing for the following week.

The Monday morning class was a bit of a handful, but that was to be expected with a room full of freshmen on their first day. I was honestly surprised how few came in late for a class scheduled at eight in the morning. It usually took a few weeks for incoming freshmen to find their groove, and I tried to keep that in mind when planning. Many of my colleagues loathed a room full of freshmen, but I tried to be empathetic. Most of these kids weren't properly prepared to be out on their own.

The only real downside to the morning was my new nickname, Professor Daddy. Maybe if the name slipped out of a certain blonde's lips I would be more accepting, but hearing my students whisper it was a whole different matter. My one hope was that the love letters would not be a thing this year. It was hard to be flattered by the attention when it could very well cost me my job. I already had enough on my plate.

With any luck, the newest educator would take some of the attention off me. Professor Zack Porter was added to the History department this year and word around campus was that he paid for his education by modeling. The students were going to eat him alive.

There was a slight spring in my step as I headed to my second class of the day. Most students who took Creative Writing had a genuine passion for it. Having students who want to be in your class is a completely different beast than those who need to be there because of a graduation requirement. The cherry on top was a smaller class size. With only ten students, I could give each of them significantly more attention than that of a class double the size.

Small classes weren't common at Pine Grove University. This one was actually more of an overflow. The last three semesters it had been booked within minutes. Professor Carlton was heading the full class this semester, leaving me with a dream-sized group.

I was pleasantly surprised when I walked through the door ten minutes before class and some of my students were already seated. Punctuality after lunch was a good sign. Gathered in a cluster, they were deep in conversation about the summer. Due to their positioning, I was unsure of the number of students present.

"Hello class," I greeted them as I walked over to the desk at the front.

"Hello, Professor Grant," a cheery voice called out. Valerie Davis. I had her as a student in a few of my prior classes. She was a sweet girl who thankfully never hit on me, but she was a bit of a suck-up.

I started removing my supplies from my bag when a familiar voice caught my attention.

"I spent the summer waiting tables at the Hot Wingz and Thighs and then took a trip to Florida with some friends."

My body froze as the familiar, lithe voice danced around me. There was no way. What were the odds *she* would be here?

My skin felt itchy. My clothing was too tight. I tried to swallow, but my mouth had gone dry. My pulse was racing, and I felt dizzy. I needed to get myself together. Closing my eyes, I took a few deep breaths.

Come on Joshua, don't pass out in front of her. Or the rest of the class.

I was a mess.

All it took was her voice to send me spiraling out of control. The worst part was that I didn't know if I was terrified or elated. Was it possible to be both at the same time?

After a few more deep breaths, I felt calm enough to look up. None of the class seemed to notice my panic. Small miracles. They were still huddled in deep conversation.

A new emotion crept its way inside me: anger. She hadn't noticed me yet. Did she not recognize my voice? I know we hadn't spoken much that night, but it was more than enough to remember me. I remembered hers. It was seared into my soul.

"Okay, everyone. Why don't we go ahead and take our seats?" I suggested after two more students walked in. My voice was calm, but my fists were balled tightly.

Everyone parted from the group to find an open desk. That was when I saw her. She looked different, but it was definitely her. The crinkled blonde beach waves were now smooth and styled in a high ponytail. Her face was done up instead of the fresh sun's glow. The blouse she wore was quite flattering and the skirt... I couldn't see much because of the desk, but her beautiful legs were on display underneath. And God help me, was she wearing stilettos?

I quickly averted my gaze, not wanting to be caught staring. Just that quick peek was enough to fill my mind with the lewdest thoughts. I wanted to bend her over the desk and spank her tight ass for tempting me. Then I wanted to fuck her senseless until she forgot about the pain.

What was wrong with me? How was I supposed to teach a class with her in it?

I raked a hand through my hair as I reached for my roster. It hadn't gone unnoticed that she still wasn't reacting to my presence. Her expression was neutral, unreadable, and it made me simmer with a slow rage.

"Welcome everyone to Creative Writing. For those who haven't had a class with me before, I am Professor Grant." I introduced myself to the class with a smile. My voice was calm as I hid the anguish I felt beneath the surface.

A few of the students said hello, but my summer fling sat silent. She wasn't even looking at me like the others. Instead, her attention was on a sheet of paper placed on her desk. It felt like salt was being dumped on an open wound. She was ignoring me on purpose.

That was perfectly fine, I tried to tell myself. Honestly, it was what I should be doing. She was my student. I may not have known that when we met, but I knew that now. Except, the rationalization was doing nothing to calm my damaged pride.

Look at me.

I needed her to acknowledge me. I craved her affirmation. It was like that night all over again when all I asked for was her name. My hand tightened on the list of names as a smile crossed my lips. I was the one in charge now.

Ten names were printed on the roster I held and one of them was hers. There were a few ways I could narrow down her name. The most obvious was taking roll, but I wanted to make her say it. I wanted her to look at me and give me what I wanted.

"To start things off, I'm going to take roll. Since we are such a small class, I get the unique opportunity to get to know each of you a little better. We will go around the room. Stand up, introduce yourself, and tell me what year you are in." She wouldn't be able to deny me now.

"We will start here." I pointed to a young man with shaggy blonde hair and an athletic build.

He stood up with a cool confidence that told me he was no stranger to being the center of attention. I used to be like that. Mr. Swagger gave the other students a mischievous grin, winking in the direction of my blonde obsession and the girl who sat next to her. I held in my scowl as they both smiled in response.

"Hello, I'm Jonathan Bailey and I'm a junior. I actually transferred here this year from Ohio State," he said, immediately taking his seat.

"Welcome to Pine Grove University, Jonathan. I hope you enjoy your time here." Just not with her.

Each student stood one by one, the anticipation growing as I got closer to her. I gave each one my full attention despite the magnetism I kept feeling to stare her way.

Finally, it was her turn. My anguish would soon be over. As she stood and took a step forward, I got my first look at her outfit. The beautiful cream blouse was paired with a tight pencil skirt that stopped mid-thigh. The stiletto heels showed off her beautifully toned legs.

I fought the urge to fall to my knees so I could plant a kiss on those small ankles, working my way up to bury my face between her thighs. Jesus Christ, I was going to have an erection in front of the class.

"Hi, everyone," she said with a small wave and a beautiful smile. "My name is Cassidy Jones, but everyone calls me Cassie. This is my third year here at PGU."

Cassie. A beautiful name. I should have been thrilled to finally have her name. Instead, I felt frustrated. She purposely made eye contact with each student as she spoke, but she never looked my way. Why was she going to such lengths to intentionally ignore me? Was it because she realized she slept with her professor, or had I really done something wrong that night?

Acknowledge me, damn it!

"Thank you, Cassie," I said, forcing a smile. Her name rolled off my lips far too easily. Inside, I was a twisted knot of disappointment and frustration. The reality of our situation was crushing me.

After the last student introduced themself, I resigned myself to my fate. Whatever had been there that night was obviously gone, if it had ever really been there. I needed to move on. Cassie had.

"I hope everyone enjoys writing because you will be doing a lot of it," I said as I passed out the syllabus. "A few things I want to make clear from the beginning. First, grammar and spelling. Points will be taken off for your grammatical mistakes. Nothing pulls a reader out of the moment like errors. I am more lenient on assignments written in class, though. My office hours are at the bottom of the syllabus along with my email. I cannot stress this enough. Please reach out in advance for an appointment. Not everything requires us to meet in person. I try to leave that time for those who truly need it."

That last bit was a complete lie. Pre-scheduling appointments was something I came up with a while ago to weed out the young girls who wasted my time trying to flirt with me. While some of the creative excuses were amusing, it got old pretty fast.

Every girl was staring up at me with the same dreamy look. Every girl except Cassie. Her focus was solely on the syllabus, not bothering to raise her head once. The behavior was almost childish. Maybe she would just drop the class after today, and then I would be free of her.

But did I really want to be free of her?

"Today, I want to get to know your voice. You have until the end of class to write your paper. No pressure on this one. I just want to get a feel for where everyone is at. I know everything is digital today, so I have pens and paper up here for anyone who needs it. Once you're done, place your work on the desk and leave." No one grumbled at the assignment. That was a good sign. "Your theme is eye contact. Any kind of story. Any genre. It doesn't matter. Show me what you can do."

With that, I sat down at the front desk and pulled out one of my journals to do some writing of my own. A few of the students approached the desk, silently grabbing supplies, but I didn't bother acknowledging them, already lost in my own thoughts.

There was a time when I wanted to be a professional writer. If you asked me when I changed my mind, I wouldn't be able to give you a straight answer. I used to stay up late in middle school crafting elaborate, although cringeworthy, stories. In high school, I joined the school paper. It didn't matter what I was writing, just that I was writing.

When I arrived at college, things changed so gradually that I didn't even notice it. A little voice in the back of my mind took hold, filling me with self-doubt. The closer to graduation, the louder the voice became. Could I really make a living this way?

Everyone assumed I suddenly found a passion for education. My actual reason was that phrase, "those who can't, teach." Teaching seemed like a more reliable income. My passion for teaching showed itself midway through my first year. Seeing the students improve under my guidance made me feel like I was saving them from my fate.

I still spent a lot of my time writing. It was one of my favorite hobbies. The fear still gripped me, though, and held me back from letting my projects see the light of day. It was a smaller voice than it used to be, but it was still there.

It was the same voice that made me second-guess myself after Janet. I always knew I was attractive. I never had a problem getting a date in college, or even high school. The legion of college girls that fawned over me every year was more than enough proof as the years went on that I still had it. When Janet dumped me with no explanation, I was left to flounder amongst the *what-ifs* of it all. The new rejection from Cassie was only further proof that I wasn't enough.

Writing was my escape. I may no longer have the confidence to share my work, but I still find peace in the creation aspect. Giving my thoughts and ideas a physical form is cathartic, and journaling has become the most powerful outlet for me. If I let the words spill from me, then I can be free of all the self-doubt.

"It looks like you had a fun summer, Professor Grant. I don't think I have ever seen you so tan." Valerie Davis stood in front of my desk with a bold smile. Her red ringlets bounced as she tilted her head to the side with a mischievous look.

"That I did," I confirmed without elaborating. No matter how innocent the question, I kept my private life as vague as possible with students.

Looking past her, I noticed the classroom was otherwise empty. I had been so engrossed in my writing that I didn't even notice when the others left. This was why I normally didn't indulge in my personal writing during class.

"Well, I am really excited to have you again this year, Professor Grant," Valerie said, pulling my attention back to her. Her green eyes locked on me as she waited for my response. This was not quite the behavior I was used to from her.

"I'm glad, Valerie. It is always a pleasure to have you as a student," I offered, not entirely sure why she was still standing in front of me. "See you on Wednesday."

The awkward silence gave me the same uncomfortable feeling as nails scraping down a chalkboard. I could feel my skin crawl. Ready to end whatever this moment was, I gave her a polite smile and packed my things, hoping she would take a hint.

"See you Wednesday, *Professor Grant*."

Nope. I did not like how she said my name just then. I kept my head down as I left the room, refusing to acknowledge what had just happened.

Fuck.

Episode 4
Chili Dogs and Regrets

Joshua

A chili dog from Sal's with a side of onion rings and a cold beer, the dinner of champions. My original plan was something healthier, but after the day's events, I wanted some greasy comfort food at its finest.

I sat down at my dining room table and took a bite, savoring the way the cheese and beef blended with the sweet and spicy chili. Sal's had the best freaking chili dogs in town, and I would gladly fight anyone who said otherwise. The long, deep moan of enjoyment that escaped me would have been embarrassing if anyone else was around to hear it. Maybe eating by myself wasn't the end of the world.

I had spent most of my relationship sharing dinner every night with Janet. We used to pop open a bottle of wine and spend the evenings cooking together. I barely had time to acclimate to the solitude before Eddie whisked me away to Florida, where we had almost every meal together.

Coming back home had been a rude awakening. The crushing silence of that first night back nearly destroyed me. I ended up skipping dinner, choosing to spend the night consumed with my loneliness. Now, I was sitting alone making sex noises while I ate. I guess that could be considered progress.

I took my time indulging in the simple pleasure of eating. If this was going to be my life for the foreseeable future, then I needed to get used to being alone.

After dinner, I grabbed another beer and sat down with the assignments from Creative Writing. A very small part of me was excited to read what Cassie had written. It was a chance to gain some insight into her beyond her knack for giving orders.

The first paper was by Bill Cooper. I pulled out a pen and pad to make notes as I read through the story. It was a spy thriller of sorts, and not bad considering the time constraints. There was still room for improvement, of course. After combing through it two more times, I was fairly satisfied with my notes.

I repeated the process with each paper. Some stories were definitely more memorable than others. Jonathan wrote a captivating narrative about a childhood memory. I wanted to hate him after his flirtations with Cassie, but the boy had talent. Valerie's paper was a bit on the safe side. I had been expecting something more daring and less generic, considering the caliber of work I was used to reading from her.

My hands trembled when I read the name on the next paper: Cassidy Jones.

Cassie.

I pulled the paper closer, hoping to discover the scent of cherries and vanilla. Of course, it only smelled like paper. She would not have rubbed her writing assignment all over her body in the middle of class. That would have been absolutely insane. Still, the disappointment crept its way over me.

I was the insane one sniffing writing assignments. And why? To chase after someone off-limits? Cassie was my student. I was her professor. What we did should never have happened. If Cassie could act like an adult and move on, then I could, too.

Turning my attention to the paper, I began to do my job and read it.

A few lines in, I recognized her story. It was about a young woman who went to a bar and was approached by an older man. The story was clearly about us.

Intoxicating excitement bubbled up inside of me. My beautiful Cassie was acknowledging me. It still didn't explain the harsh brush-off she gave me in class, but I could no longer be mad. This felt like a gift.

She wrote about us!

Wait. She wrote about... us... Fuck.

Cassie turned in an official assignment about me picking her up at a bar. The sense of dread that washed over me drained all of my newfound happiness. I felt sick. Maybe the chili dog had not been a great idea.

I tried to calm myself. This might not be as bad as I thought. Surely she wasn't foolish enough to put my name on paper. I took a calming breath and continued reading.

If nothing else, I was getting the privilege of experiencing that night through Cassie's eyes. She was quite flattering in her description of me, which filled me with a satisfying warmth.

> *Those piercing, brown eyes looked at*
> *me just as warmly as his smile, but*
> *I could see the hunger behind them.*
> *It made my panties wet knowing he*
> *wanted me.*

My mouth dried as I realized this wasn't just a normal meet-cute kind of story. Cassie had written about *everything*. The further into the story I read, the more my anxiety blended with arousal.

> *He dropped to his knees before me,*
> *ready to worship me with his mouth.*
> *I was so eager for the pleasure he*
> *was about to give me. My excite-*
> *ment soaked through the fabric bar-*
> *rier that separated us.*

The whole paper was an extremely erotic account of our night. I sat there wide-eyed after reading it. The professor in me actually wanted to grade the damn thing. With some editing, the paper would be a great submission to a *gentleman's* magazine.

Dear Penthouse,

I slept with my professor.

The depraved man inside me read it again. I pulled out my cock and stroked it. Her naughty words called to me, reminding me how good it all felt. I couldn't resist.

It was like I was back kneeling before her. My body was reacting to the memories of her. Drowning in the phantom scent of cherries and vanilla, I licked the memory of her cunt off my lips.

> *His tongue expertly swirled around my clit while his finger pumped inside me. The electrifying pleasure that coursed through me consumed my body. This man was sent down from the gods above just to service me with orgasms.*

My eyes fell shut as my own orgasm approached. It was the memory of her climax, the way she spasmed and screamed, that sent me over the edge. My cock pulsed as white, hot ropes splattered over a page of her paper.

"Fuck me," I muttered, immediately recognizing how messed up my little spank fest was.

I stood up and grabbed a napkin, but my efforts were wasted. Even though I could salvage most of the paper, I couldn't hand it back to her with a faint cum stain. In all my years, I had never masturbated to a student's assignment. This was too much. I had no self-control.

The inevitable shame crashed over me and drowned me with my disgust. Cassie was my student. This could not happen. I needed to be the adult and fix it.

I opened my laptop and drafted a brief email. The moment I hit send, I regretted it. Demanding she come to my office was not a great idea, but I didn't have a choice. I didn't want her to get in trouble.

I just needed her to drop the class so I wouldn't have to report her. Cassie would understand.

Episode 5

Another Day in Paradise

Cassie

I stared at the email from Professor Grant with a growing sense of unease. It was vague and ominous. There was no warmth in it at all.

> *Cassidy,*
>
> *Please come to my office at 5 p.m. to discuss the assignment you turned in.*
>
> *Professor Grant*

Why did I write that stupid paper? It seemed like a great idea in the heat of the moment. I was trying to be sexy. Maybe it appeared desperate instead. I just couldn't help myself.

That entire class was an exercise in self-restraint. The moment he walked through that door, I realized I was in over my head. He looked even hotter in his button-down shirt and slacks than he did the night we met. Something about a man dressed professionally always gets me going. I had to avert my eyes the entire time he spoke because I was terrified of what I might do if we made eye contact.

"The email isn't going to magically say something else, no matter how many times you read it," Nicole teased.

I looked up from my phone with a frown. Nicole, my best friend and roommate, was standing in the kitchen with a cup of coffee in hand, looking at me with pity. She didn't need to read over my shoulder to know what I was looking at. I had been fretting over the stupid thing since I saw it last night.

"This is all your fault," I moaned in frustration.

"I only helped you pick out your outfit. I didn't tell you to do whatever you did to piss off Professor Daddy, hun."

Nicole didn't know about what I wrote, or that I had already met Professor Grant in Florida. Not that I knew at the time that the man eating me like I was ambrosia in a bathroom was Pine Grove University's resident hot professor. All she knew was I had one of his classes this semester.

It still felt easy to blame Nicole. She had unknowingly set the entire chain of events in motion when she suggested we go out for drinks that night, only to leave me alone when a hot lifeguard asked to take her for a moonlit walk on the beach. I was all alone and ready to make some bad decisions.

Honestly, the only reason I agreed to hook up with anyone that night was to test the waters. There was a pattern in my past relationships. I was always the one taking orders and making concessions. For once, I wanted to be the one in charge. When the handsome older man offered to buy me a drink, I figured he was the perfect test subject.

I didn't find out my bathroom hookup was my professor until I got home. Nicole and I were comparing our schedules for the semester, and she freaked out when I said his name. The look she gave me when I admitted I had never seen a picture of the infamous Professor Grant... you would have thought I sprouted a second head.

Nicole wasted no time pulling up a picture of Professor Grant from the university's website. I almost choked on my soda when I realized he was the same man I watched masturbate. Nicole just thought I was in shock because he was so attractive.

"I know, but I am not ready to take responsibility for my actions," I continued to complain.

"Maybe it won't be that bad, hun. Or maybe he wants to kiss a little ass because you're a legacy student," she said with a wink.

My cheeks blushed at the thought of Professor Grant on his knees kissing my ass. I shook my head, willing the dirty thoughts away. Daydreaming about my professor would not make the situation better.

"He doesn't know. None of my professors this term know yet." It was only a matter of time until they found out, and then things would get weird. They always did once my professors realized who my family was.

"Then that means you aren't getting any special treatment, so you can't be late. C'mon, Cassie," Nicole called out from the door.

With a huff, I grabbed my stuff and headed out.

I was in a daze walking to my Modern American Literature class. That stupid email was all I could think about. The idea of being alone with Professor Grant was both frightening and thrilling. He was asking to meet in his office alone after his scheduled office hours. Well, he didn't ask so much as tell me which was a behavior that needed correcting.

Maybe he wanted an encore. I could be walking into an attempted seduction, a bit of sex on his desk. I had never done anything like that before.

Completely lost in my Professor Grant fantasies, I didn't notice the person standing right in my path until my face crashed into their firm chest.

"Cassie?" a familiar voice asked.

Looking up, my cheeks flushed as I locked eyes with one of the guys from Creative Writing. The one who was the embodiment of an all-American boy next door and had winked at me in class.

"I'm so sorry! Jonathan, right?" I stuttered in embarrassment.

He took a step back, running a hand through his blonde hair as he checked me out. A shiver of lust ran through me as his gaze caressed my body.

Attention from men is something I have struggled to accept. I spent much of my teens invisible to everyone. Even now, I am not a natural beauty. If my journey from ugly duckling to swan has taught me anything, it is that society's idea of natural beauty doesn't exist. Makeup is a powerful tool.

My fingers fidgeted nervously, unsure how to proceed after plowing into him. The hungry look and golden-boy smile did little to ease the tension. It only took a little embarrassment to throw me completely off-balance.

"No worries, Cassie. It was my fault for standing here." He laughed with a shrug. "Are you on your way to MAL with Professor Martin, by any chance?"

"Yes, I am. I guess we have a few classes together." My confidence returned, and I stood a little straighter.

"After you," Jonathan insisted, opening the door.

Sitting in the front always felt like everyone was watching me while sitting in the back felt like I wasn't a part of the class. Lucky for me, there were plenty of seats open in the middle. As soon as I took my seat, Jonathan planted himself in the empty one to my right.

He leaned toward me, grinning with excitement. "I haven't had the chance to make many friends since moving here. Maybe, since we are going to be seeing a lot of each other anyway, we could hang out sometime?"

Jonathan was asking me on a date. He didn't explicitly say it was a date, but I knew how to read between the lines. Unfortunately for Jonathan, I was currently hung up on someone else. The only thing I was available for was friendship.

"That would be cool. I could introduce you to some of my other friends. My best friend, Nicole, would love you," I offered.

The carefree smile he had been sporting since we started talking faltered for just the briefest moment. It made me feel guilty, even though I did nothing wrong.

"Give me your phone real quick. Let me plug in my number," I offered, extending my hand while making a grabbing motion, hoping to ease the guilt.

Jonathan passed me his phone without hesitation. I typed my name and number into his contacts. Then I snapped a quick selfie.

"Um, are you taking a selfie with my phone?" Jonathan asked, more amused than confused.

"Sure am. Just going to set this beauty as the pic under my contact," I explained as I typed a few buttons.

After sending a quick text to my phone so I would have his number, I handed it back. His bright smile was beaming again, wiping away the guilt I felt before. I know I was probably leading him on, but I could fix that later.

Episode 6
Summoned

Cassie

My hands trembled as I stood outside Professor Grant's office. There was a heavy weight pressing on my chest that made each breath a struggle. The fear of the unknown was crushing me. I placed my hand on the wooden frame to steady myself.

Breathe.

It felt strange to be standing here with no one else around. I couldn't tell if the other professors were hidden away in their offices like Professor Grant or simply gone for the day. Had Professor Grant arranged for us to meet when no one else was around? The thought gave me a small thrill.

With a deep inhale, I filled my lungs with the stale air around me and held it as I found my center. Slowly, I released the breath, letting my anxiety out with it.

There was no reason to let myself get worked up like this. I shouldn't just assume this was about something bad.

Except that you handed in a very detailed event of your night together as a class assignment. The doubt taunted me, but I quickly shut it down. He had been an eager participant during our little bathroom fling. In fact, *he* had approached *me*. Offering to buy a girl a drink has never been an innocent gesture.

Suck it up, Cassie. I just needed to face this head on.

Turning the knob, I opened the door and entered the office without bothering to knock. It may have been rude on my part, but so was the way his email summoned me like I was supposed to drop everything on his whim.

I should have emailed him back declining to meet, or countered his offer with a different time. That night in the bar had been a huge step forward in finding my voice. I had found my power, and it felt amazing. This felt like the opposite of that. I hated the idea that I had rolled over so easily. Him being my professor was no excuse.

All my regrets were pointless once I entered his office, though. I was already here and time machines didn't exist. All I could do was promise myself to be better with my boundaries going forward.

Professor Grant looked absolutely delicious sitting at his desk. The way his sleeves were rolled up his forearms filled me with need. I wanted those arms wrapped around me in a tight embrace while I ground my hips into him.

My thighs rubbed together as desire pooled between my legs. An image of that night flashed through my mind: Professor Grant standing in front of me and stroking his cock eagerly for my approval. The high of that moment was amazing. It was hard to believe the man in front of me was the same person.

Head down, Professor Grant's attention was on the pages of a leather-bound journal he feverishly wrote in. His body hunched over and rigid as he closed himself off to the rest of the world. There was an intensity in his focus on that notebook, like his soul was spilling out on those pages. The stress radiated off of him in waves.

My body urged me to reach out and calm whatever storm was brewing inside of him, knowing that I somehow had that power. But I didn't move. He had not earned my comfort, and I was still pissed off, even if it hurt me to see him so clearly distressed.

"Professor Grant," I greeted with a smile, tired of waiting for him to notice my presence.

Startled, Professor Grant looked up from his desk tensely, which was not an encouraging reaction. He shouldn't look like a deer in headlights when he was the one who invited me. My smile widened as I tried to hide my growing irritation and anxiety. I needed to portray all the confidence I definitely wasn't feeling.

Fake it till you make it, baby.

His eyes zeroed in on my hands as I tugged at my skirt, the only outward sign of my nerves. Those brown eyes trailed down my legs with the same hunger I recognized from our night. Professor Grant seemed to forget that he was not hidden while he feasted on the sight of me.

Being watched with such intense need felt empowering. I was wanted, desired. Even though I knew I could make this man obey me, seeing the evidence again gave me the genuine confidence I so desperately needed.

Then our eyes met. The color drained from Professor Grant's face as he realized he had been caught. I couldn't help my little smirk in response, needing to rub it in. He cleared his throat while he shuffled things around, trying to look at anything but me.

I was taking too much pleasure in his discomfort. Watching him squirm turned me on. Part of me wanted to push his buttons, amplify the humiliation he felt, but I refrained. Until I knew why I had been summoned, I needed to behave.

"Cassie. Um, thank you for coming. Please have a seat," Professor Grant offered while still avoiding eye contact. He gestured towards the chair in front of his large, wooden desk.

No. Something about sitting in that small chair while he looked down on me from the other side of his desk felt like I would be submitting to him. I didn't like that power dynamic.

"I'll stand. Thank you," I said in my sweetest voice. There was no way I was letting him call the shots right now.

"Right. Well, this will be quick. I think considering our... situation that it would be best if you dropped the class."

Professor Grant's words felt like a punch to the gut. He wanted me to drop the class? I was vaguely aware that the mask of my sunny disposition was cracking because of my professor's frowning face.

"I just don't think being your professor is a good idea, especially after the assignment you turned in." Professor Grant continued, but his words faded into the background.

If I were thinking rationally, I would have seen his request as reasonable. We had fooled around in a random bathroom over summer break. Then, I recounted the moment on paper as a student in his class and turned it in. I should have been grateful he wasn't reporting me to the dean.

The problem was, I could not think rationally right now. He wanted me to drop the class, and I couldn't, not even if I wanted to. It was not an option, ever. The worst part was that I couldn't even tell him that without complicating things more.

My pulse raced as my mind tried to fight through the panic and think up a solution. The walls closed in around me as my world began to fall apart. Aunt Margaret would demand answers, as would Gram. Everything promised to me would be ripped away.

Then it came to me, a truly desperate idea. If I failed, I risked suspension, but I was already about to lose it all. This was my only option.

"Cassie?" My name dripped with concern as it fell from Professor Grant's lips.

His voice pulled me back from the edge into the present. An eerie calm fell over me. I made this man bend to my will once before. I could do it again.

"No."

"No?" His eyes widened in shock, obviously not expecting my response.

"No. I will not be dropping your class, Professor Grant." My eyes bore into his as I stood my ground.

The air felt heavy, like a thick fog of tension surrounding us. We were in a battle of wills staring each other down and demanding the other submit. Only, Professor Grant did not seem nearly as confident. His expression was one more of pain than determination.

Testing the waters, I took a step forward, watching Professor Grant brace himself. If I didn't know any better, I would think my professor was afraid of me. The feeling did not sit well with me. I wasn't after fear.

A few more cautious steps put me right next to his desk. This close, I could clearly see signs of an internal struggle. The muscles in his face seemed to strain to hold his neutral expression. The pain behind his eyes was undeniable. It broke my heart.

Instinctively, I reached out to comfort my poor, tormented professor. His body stiffened as he tried to press further back in his chair.

"Please... I can't." The plea came out strained.

The man before seemed very different from the one I met that night, less excitement and confidence. I wanted the man from before. I needed the man from before if this was going to work.

Ignoring him, I continued my quest to comfort him. Sweet surrender painted his expression the moment my hand cupped the side of his face. Professor Grant nuzzled into my palm with closed eyes as all the fight drained from his body.

His shoulders dropped their tension. A low hum of contentment vibrated through him as I lightly stroked my thumb against his cheek. It was a heady feeling having this man melt so easily under my touch.

Those beautiful brown eyes opened. Gone was the pain and fear. Instead, a predator was staring back at me with a look of pure hunger. He bit his bottom lip, then released it into a sinfully delicious smile. Those lips called to me and tempted me to taste.

My eyes lingered on his mouth as I ran my tongue along my lips in response.

I realized my mistake too late. The only warning I had was his low growl of need before the professor pounced.

Fingers tangled in the back of my hair, holding me in place with a firm grasp. Struggling only seemed to encourage him, which I didn't mind. I liked it rough.

Professor Grant's mouth crashed into mine, kissing me with complete abandon. His tongue forced its way past my lips, unwilling to yield. A small whimper escaped as I gave into the fiery kiss.

The feral need that had overcome Professor Grant was contagious. It filled my veins with unbridled lust, leaving my panties soaked. I needed him closer. I needed more.

My legs parted, allowing the professor to grind against my core. Even with the clothing between us, I could feel how hard he was for me. It was torture having his thick erection so close but not filling me.

A warm hand worked its way under my cami, leaving a trail of goosebumps over my skin as he explored. When his fingertips reached the lace of my bra, a sobering realization came over me. I was letting Professor Grant be in control.

As much as I needed his touch, it couldn't be like this, especially not right after he tried to reject me. Professor Grant would not be let off the hook for his behavior so easily.

Pulling back from his kiss was a challenge. My body fought against me, not wanting to break the connection. It took everything in me to create a fraction of space between us.

Panting for breath, I whispered a single word that froze Professor Grant in place.

"Stop."

Episode 7

You Can Do a Lot in Ten Seconds

Joshua

Maybe ten seconds had passed, but those ten seconds were filled with panic as I stood in shock. Cassie was here. She offered herself to me so willingly, then uttered the worst possible word. *Stop.* But I didn't want to stop, not when my Cassie was before me with her legs spread so invitingly. I hated the word more than anything else in the world at that moment.

You're failing again.

No. No. No. Not again! I couldn't let it end like last time. It drove me crazy enough when I thought I would never see her again. Now? Knowing she was here on campus? I would never know peace again without Cassie's sweet touch.

Ten seconds ticked away as I racked my brain trying to figure out where I went wrong. Everything until she uttered that cursed word led me to believe that Cassie wanted this. She wrote a paper about me worshiping her body and turned it in as a class assignment. That was obviously a cry for my attention. She initiated the touching in my office only moments ago. And then when I snapped, her body responded to my lust. God, how she responded. That fucking whimper was my new favorite sound.

Focus.

The paper! Maybe there was something she had written that would help me. Lord knows I read the thing enough times. Even this morning, I had shamefully jerked myself to her words, as I longed to relive that night. The shame that came after each orgasm didn't seem to deter me one bit. I was on a constant mission to reclaim that high.

Frantically, I replayed the scene she had written, desperate to salvage the moment. The panic was drowning me, but I pushed through it. There had to be something that was useful. My breath stilled as I scanned my memories for anything that could help me. The longest ten seconds of my entire life ticked as I drove myself mad.

And then it came to me in a moment of clarity. I took a long breath, purging the fear from my body as I exhaled. The answer was right in front of me the entire time, but I was too caught up in my own hysteria to see it.

My body dropped to the ground as I knelt before Cassie. She instantly straightened her posture as she took notice of my surrender. Those beautiful lips formed a small smile, rewarding my behavior. The spark of desire in her eyes didn't go unnoticed as I tried my best to appear subservient. My beautiful goddess wanted the feel of control.

Cassie looked like a queen perched on my desk as she peered down at me. The confidence that radiated from her left me in awe. This woman was truly worthy of being worshiped, but not in the traditional sense. I wanted to express my devotion to her in a sinfully carnal way.

The thought of erotic worship sent my body into overdrive. My dick was hard, pressing against my pants as it begged for release. Control, I needed control.

Not trusting myself to be good, my hands clasped together. It was frustrating to have Cassie so close without my hands all over her, but I had to endure it. The sooner I could convince her I would be compliant, the sooner I could reap the rewards.

It was the third read through last night that I noticed there was a theme to her paper, submission and worship. It was sprinkled throughout her story with some interesting word choices that I just assumed were clever flourishes. Honestly, I should have caught on sooner.

"I am so sorry. Forgive me." The words came out between heavy breaths as I forced myself to keep in control. I would not ruin this now that I was so close.

"Do you think you deserve forgiveness?" Cassie's words cut through me like a knife, and I couldn't hide the wince.

What was it about this girl that had me so tied up in knots? The idea that I had somehow displeased her was physically painful. My body and mind reacting like this was new territory that I didn't know how to navigate.

"No, not yet," I confessed, hopeful I could still turn this around somehow. I needed my sun to keep shining her beautiful light down on me. I didn't want to be in the dark anymore.

Cassie's legs were still parted with me between them. My current position gave me a perfect view up her skirt. It was a battle to keep my eyes on her face and not the lacy panties she was wearing. She had to have worn them with me in mind, and that little realization had me fighting back a groan.

"You summoned me. That wasn't very nice," she chastised me. Despite the annoyed tone, her expression was not serious.

I was clearly being tested, which meant I had to be careful with how I responded. Not entirely sure what to do, I gently placed a hand on her calf and guided it to my lips. With eyes closed, I planted a chaste kiss on her ankle, hoping to smooth things over.

"My apologies. A goddess should never be summoned," I whispered against her skin.

Internally, I cringed at how awful that was. Thinking on my knees was not my specialty. If I was lucky, Cassie would be too inexperienced to realize how bad that sounded.

Looking up, I tried to gauge her response. She appeared awestruck, which was better than her earlier frustration. Maybe I was not as bad at this as I thought.

A warm glow filled me as she gazed down at me. The pressure that had been suffocating me finally dissipated. My whole body relaxed, and I felt like I could breathe again. Cassie truly was my goddess, the only one who could bring me peace.

The relief was short-lived as a frown formed again. Those beautiful lips parted, ready to continue torturing me. "I'm not dropping the class. I mean it."

Reality crashed down on me like a pile of bricks raining from the sky. My mouth went dry and my chest tightened as a new panic made its home inside me. Cassie was a student. My student. Kneeling on the floor, ready to worship her sinful body with my own, was wrong for so many reasons. The whole reason for summoning her was to put an end to it.

Except… I didn't want it to end. My body craved her and the carnal pleasures it was denied during our first encounter. No matter how desperate I was for Cassie, I had to fight this feeling. I was the adult in this situation. I needed to—

"Stop thinking and look at me," Cassie barked. The harsh tone pulled me out of my head.

"What?" I blinked a few times in shock. Never had she sounded so hard when commanding me. My shoulders slumped inward as my body ached from her scolding.

"You look like you are upsetting yourself. That won't do. Whatever you were thinking about, just stop. I forbid it." Her brows were pinched together with concern as she gave her command.

"Cassie, things—"

"Nope," she bluntly shut me down, shaking her head.

I grew increasingly frustrated with her behavior. Being told no was getting old. As much as I loathed to admit it, it was the only part that was getting under my skin. I didn't mind Cassie giving me orders like I thought I would. There was something fun and freeing about handing over control, and the feeling her praise gave me was addictive. I found myself eager to hear her say good boy. My only frustration was her repeated use of the word no. It made whatever this was dangerous.

"I can have you removed, Cassie," I threatened calmly. It was a complete bluff. I was far too infatuated to follow through with the threat, but I couldn't let her know. Cassie had to be the one to pull the plug and set me free.

She didn't look impressed by my threat, probably because I was still kneeling with her ankle in my hand. At some point, I had begun to trace small circles with my thumb over her skin. While touching her brought me a clarity I had been missing lately, it undermined my attempt to control the situation.

At what point had I lost all control? This was a bigger mess than I realized. I couldn't even bring myself to stand now. I was still holding on to some deranged hope this would magically work itself out if I behaved for my darling Cassie.

"This can go one of two ways because I am *not* dropping your class," Cassie said, pulling her leg from my grasp. "You can either spend every Monday and Wednesday in close proximity to me knowing only you can touch me, or you can spend them wondering who has been exploring my body instead of you. The choice is yours."

An image of that one punk that winked at her flashed in my mind, Jonathan something. I imagined him openly flirting with Cassie, *my Cassie,* right in front of me during class. Would she let him touch her? Let him do things to her I have not been allowed to do?

My blood boiled as unbridled rage set in. There was a throbbing in my fingers as my fists tightened. The image of their naked bodies writhing together in pleasure taunted me. I could not survive that torture.

"You're mine," I growled as I leaped to my feet. My hands grabbed the desk, caging her between my arms so she couldn't escape. "Mine," I whispered, feeling feral and unhinged.

I had never felt so out of control in my life, but Cassie was threatening to torture me. Even my suggestion of distance felt completely insane now that she had spoon fed me the idea of her with other men.

Cassie was mine to serve and worship. No one else would be allowed to bask in her light, only me.

Cassie leaned in and reached between my legs to stroke me to fullness. My head fell to her shoulder as I groaned with contentment and my ragged breath slowed. Her touch felt so good even if it was over my pants. How could I have thought even for one second of giving this up?

"Good boy," Cassie cooed softly. "You made the right choice."

Too wrapped up in the way she was rubbing me, I didn't immediately respond to her praise. I had been starving for her since the first night. This little crumb was heaven, and I wanted to enjoy it for as long as possible.

"This is going to be on my terms. Do you understand, Professor Grant?" Cassie's soft voice washed over me, pulling me further into heavenly submission.

"Joshua. My name is Joshua," I replied, blissed-out from her touch. I wanted to hear her say my name.

"I am well aware," her sultry voice whispered in my ear, "but Professor Grant makes me wet. You want me wet, don't you, *Professor Grant*?" Cassie punctuated her question by squeezing my cock with the perfect amount of pressure.

"Yes," I hissed with pleasure. Any scrap of resistance vanished. Cassie could ask me to do anything, and I would obey. I was in so much trouble, and I didn't care.

"Aren't things so much nicer when you act like a good boy?" She spoke to me as if I were some pet, and I played right into it, nuzzling her neck in response. Vanilla and cherries danced around me with every breath I took and lulled me further into submission.

I'll be your good boy, Cassie.

She trailed the tips of her fingers up to the waist of my pants, teasing me with the promise of more. I lifted my head to watch her delicate movements as she dipped just under the waistband. My stomach flexed from the contact. Just a little bit further and—

"I have condoms now," I blurted like some inexperienced buffoon. When did I revert to a bumbling teenager?

"That's good to know," Cassie chuckled, making me feel like an even bigger fool. "But we aren't going to fuck in your office. You haven't earned something that risky."

With the moment broken, she gently pushed me back and hopped off the desk. I had to fight every single muscle in my body from throwing her back on the desk so I could ravish her until her legs were shaking from orgasm after orgasm. Cassie was in charge. I needed to obey even if it slowly killed me. And she was right. Having sex here was far too risky. We needed some place much more private.

"Phone," Cassie ordered with her hand stretched out.

I stood there like an idiot before I realized what she wanted. Our conversation so far had practically broken me, leaving me still disoriented. Reaching into my pocket, I fished out my cell and handed it over to her without a second thought.

Cassie made the cutest expressions while she rummaged through my phone. I probably should have been concerned, but I was lost in watching her. Besides, there was nothing incriminating on my phone. I wasn't stupid enough to look at porn on my cell. The only thing that could even possibly look bad was—

Fuck!

Janet. I still had lots of pictures of Janet and me on there. Also, the pathetic texts I sent after the breakup begging for her to at least talk to me. I should have deleted those when Eddie told me to, or never sent them in the first place, as Eddie so graciously pointed out each time.

"There. Now I am in your contacts. No more summoning me with cryptic messages from your university email. Okay?" Cassie said as she handed back my phone.

All I could do was nod in agreement, still coming down from my most recent wave of panic. Sensing my anxiety, Cassie leaned in close. Delicately, she placed her hand on the side of my face, guiding me towards her. My eyes closed as she initiated a soft, sensual kiss. Her tongue coaxed me into a gentle surrender, easing all the anxiety from me.

"You're mine now," Cassie whispered on my lips as she broke the kiss.

"All yours," I agreed.

Pleased with my confirmation, my Cassie said her goodbyes. I wasn't ready for her to go, but I didn't argue. She would see I could be good for her. I would be so good for her.

Left alone in my office, I was forced to come to terms with just how screwed I was. The worst part, though, was the giant smile that I couldn't wipe from my face. My darling Cassie claimed me. I was hers. To hell with the consequences. I just had to be smart about this because now that I had her, I would never give her up.

Episode 8
The Wrong One

Cassie

My legs wobbled like jelly as soon as I walked through the door. Somehow, I had managed to keep my composure during the short bus ride home, but walking over the threshold to my apartment was my limit. Now I could fall apart in the safety of my domain.

My purse dropped with a thud as I let out the breath I had been holding. The last of the tension that had been holding me up melted away. Without it, I had to fight from falling to the ground in a boneless mass.

The shock hadn't worn off yet, not completely. Professor Grant was mine! I could still feel the excitement coursing through my veins. From his lips to my ears, all mine!

Dazed by power and lust, I tried to figure out how things had escalated so quickly. You don't start out a meeting with your professor being reprimanded and end it with him claiming you. Part of me didn't believe it really happened. How many girls on campus have fantasized about something similar happening to them? I had to be the luckiest student at Pine Grove University.

The part that shocked me the most was when Professor Grant dropped to his knees unprompted. That singular moment turned my entire world upside down. Commanding the professor to his knees was intoxicating enough, but watching that man drop to the ground on his own almost short-circuited my brain. The willpower I had to channel so I wouldn't just fuck him right then and there was insane. My body desperately wanted to reward him, but I knew better.

Professor Grant tried to remove me from his class, twice. I couldn't just let that slide. My entire future was threatened. For that, the professor had to be punished even if it meant punishing me too. Besides, waiting for sex wasn't that big of a deal. I was sure it would happen sooner rather than later. Professor Grant had my number, after all. It was only a matter of time before he texted or called, begging to see me again.

I was practically dancing my way to my bedroom while daydreaming about my new pet professor. What would I do when he reached out? How much would I make him work for it? There had to be some task or obstacle to overcome that I could give him. Rewards had to be earned, after all.

I couldn't remember the last time I felt so in control of anything. I was never in the driver's seat in my relationships. Plus, Gram still had a small hold on my life thanks to that damn trust and the promises of an easier life after graduation. This was the first time I held the power, and it felt good. Really good.

"Your purse is vibrating," Nicole called from the living room.

Until that moment, I forgot she was home. I had forgotten about everything except the feel of Professor Grant's fingers on my skin.

The phantom touch of his fingers on my ankle sent a shiver through my body. Nothing had ever felt so right.

I rushed to my purse like a kid seeking the present pile under the tree on Christmas. There was no way Professor Grant was going to wait to text me after our little meeting. He was practically purring when I left.

Purse in hand, I plopped next to Nicole on the couch where she was watching some true crime show. I had never been one for them, but Nicole was obsessed.

"Someone is all smiles," she teased while I rummaged through my bag. "So things went well with *The Professor*?"

"Everything went better than expected," I replied vaguely.

Of course, I was dying to give Nicole all the details, but I wasn't sure if I should. Fooling around with your professor is the kind of thing you don't want to go around telling people. This was something that could get me in a lot of trouble. I needed to keep it on the down low for now.

Nicole didn't probe me further, but she kept a watchful eye as I pulled out my phone. All the excitement drained from my body as I read the text that was waiting for me.

Jonathan: Hey. Just wanted to see if you were free Friday night. Maybe you could show me what's fun in town.

That was not who I wanted to hear from.

"What's wrong? Your mood just did a total one-eighty," Nicole asked with concern.

The wrong guy is texting me, but I wasn't about to tell her that.

"There is this guy in a few of my classes that just transferred in from out of state. I gave him my number, thinking we could be friends, but—"

"He isn't looking for friendship?" Nicole rolled her eyes. She knew me and my old habits all too well. You can't hide being a doormat from your best friend.

"I don't think so, but I was up front when I gave him my number," I replied.

I don't know why I felt the need to defend my actions. Probably because of the guilt I was feeling. Even though I was clear with Jonathan, I still felt like I was leading him on. The old Cassie, all too willing to please others and avoid making waves, was still just below the surface. In the past, I had agreed to go on dates with guys I had previously turned down because of the guilt. It was something I was still working on.

"Ghost him," Nicole said with a wave of her hand like the answer was obvious. I wish it were that simple.

"I can't ghost him. I will still see him in class," I explained with a sigh. "Besides, he is kinda sweet. He just needs friends. Maybe you could go with me on Friday?"

"Nope. We already have plans on Friday, remember? Booze and bowling with Grace and her crew." And just like that, Nicole and Grace solved all my problems.

Grace was Nicole's older cousin. They were super close, being raised more like sisters than cousins. Due to the close friendship Nicole and I share, becoming friends with Grace was inevitable. She was the other rock in my life.

"Why don't you invite him along? If he needs friends, we can introduce him to a few people," Nicole offered, having no idea she was not helping things at all.

"Wouldn't she mind if we brought a stranger?" I argued half-heartedly.

"Grace? You know she would be thrilled," Nicole insisted. I did know that, but a girl could hope.

Bringing Jonathan along wouldn't be the worst thing. Maybe he would even meet someone who would interest him more than me. Grace hung with some beautiful people.

"Fine. I'll text him the invite," I conceded as I started typing my reply.

> **Cassie: Have plans with friends for booze and bowling Friday, but we would love to have you join us. It would be a great opportunity to introduce you to more people.**

The reply was almost immediate.

> **Jonathan: That sounds like a lot of fun. Count me in.**

Done. If only I felt happy instead of the gnawing guilt that was slowly eating me alive.

There was a time I would have been beyond excited that someone like Jonathan might be interested in me. High school me drooled over boys like him all day. The popular ones with muscles and a smile that could melt any girl's panties were my obsession then. Now? I only had one man I wanted.

The attraction to my professor was completely out of character. Not because Professor Grant wasn't attractive, because he definitely was. You would have to be blind not to see how hot he was. I have just never been attracted to power or older men. When you add the two together, I conjure up images of balding men in ill-fitting suits who leer at their secretaries. Not my thing at all.

But Professor Grant wasn't some creepy old dude playing grab ass. I mean, he did stare at me that night in Florida for longer than necessary. It was more than a little creepy. Did he think I wouldn't notice when he was literally standing right next to me? At the time, I was about two seconds away from publicly shaming him.

Then he spoke. The way he delivered such a cliché pick up line almost stumbling over himself was adorable, and the look on his face as he followed me to that bathroom. He seemed both nervous and confident at the same time. For some reason, that drew me in. I wanted to know what it would be like if we took things further.

The man surprised me. I had been skeptical about his abilities, but Professor Grant was masterful with his mouth. Most of the guys I had been with before were subpar at best. Oftentimes, they fumbled around with their tongues. The professor knew exactly what he was doing and was quite hungry to prove it.

I left the bar that night smitten. Not even the strange waitress who was staring daggers at me when I left could ruin my night. The same feeling was coursing through me now. I needed Professor Grant to reach out soon because I couldn't wait to play again.

I spent the rest of the evening in my room hitting the books. Trying to study after everything was proving to be next to impossible. I kept staring at my phone as if I could will him to message me. The lack of text notifications was mocking me.

Part of me wanted to just text him, but I couldn't bring myself to do it. What would I say? Would I come across as desperate and clingy? There was already an age difference that loomed over us. The last thing I wanted to do was draw attention to it by coming across as immature or needy, especially since I was supposed to be the one in charge. If Professor Grant figured out I wasn't normally confident and commanding, then the dynamic might change.

By nine o'clock, I decided to give up on pretending to be productive. The best way to stop myself from going insane was a good night's rest. There was less pep in my step as I got ready for bed, resigned to the notion that he wasn't going to text me.

The next day I woke up bright and early. To my frustration, there was still nothing from Professor Grant. It was beyond frustrating. When you give a guy your number, he is supposed to reach out. Right?

Fed up with waiting, I decided to take matters into my own hands. I took my sweet time getting ready, making sure my hair and makeup were perfect. Professor Grant was going to drool when he saw me, but we wouldn't be able to touch. That would be his punishment.

A devious smile crossed my lips as I opened the camera on my phone and began to pose.

Episode 9

A Picture is Worth a Thousand Words

Joshua

Cassie was going to be the death of me. It would be a glorious death full of beautiful temptation, but still death. She seemed to have a real knack for flooding my life with a heavenly sort of chaos.

When I awoke this morning, I decided to hit up my favorite coffee place for breakfast. Aside from whatever beguiling disaster I was walking into with Cassie, the first couple of days had gone well, and I wanted to reward myself. I had been all ready to head out when a text came from *Goddess*. Clever girl, not putting her real name in my phone.

I smiled the moment I saw the notification, more than eager to see what she had sent. Expecting some cute little good morning message or something about how she couldn't wait to see me in class, I was more than surprised when five pictures popped up. Very risqué pictures.

My cock stiffened as I scrolled through, inspecting each one. Cassie had obscured her face in the photo. I wondered if she knew how crazy hiding her face would make me when she sent them. Luckily, her face was the only thing that was covered. The pink lace that she was wearing was so see-through that I wouldn't consider it functional lingerie.

Was she going to be sitting in my class with this on under her clothes? If Cassie was trying to get my attention, she had it.

I tried to call her, but my attempt went straight to voicemail. I tried a few more times, and with each failed attempt, my chest tightened a little more until I couldn't breathe. It felt like Janet all over again. It made me sick. This, whatever it was, couldn't end before it had a chance to really begin.

My hand gripped the phone as I tried leaving a message one last time.

"Please don't ignore me, Cassie. Please. I just wanted to hear your voice," I begged. My words were strained from my panic.

I thought maybe the pictures were a gift, but the way she so easily shunned me made me question her motive. Cassie had me desperate to crawl on the ground and beg for her attention. She seemed to bring out that part of me so easily.

My phone buzzed, sending me into a frenzy.

Goddess: If you wanted to hear my voice, then you should have called last night. I don't have time this morning. See you in class.

I stared at the message in disbelief. Was she mad because I didn't call her last night? As far as I knew, we hadn't made any plans. If

Cassie had reached out to me yesterday, then I would have told her I already had plans.

Eddie insisted I join him and Carla for dinner at some new Thai place. They kept me out past ten, mostly out of pity. Apparently, being home alone reading papers and going over lesson plans was sad now. They never seemed to care when I was with Janet, taking my need to be alone to work sometimes at face value.

With a sigh of resignation, I crafted a text that would hopefully mend whatever this was. Cassie needed to learn to communicate. She was old enough to know I wasn't a mind reader. Being punished for something I wasn't told would not fly. At least this time involved sexy pictures.

Joshua: I was busy last night. But I would have much rather been listening to your sweet voice.

I waited for a moment and grew frustrated when she didn't immediately reply.

Joshua: I would love to see you outside of the classroom. Maybe Friday?

Goddess: I have plans Friday. Saturday?

I fought to push back the twinge of jealousy. It was a bit hypocritical to be upset at her for having plans when I was out with friends last night. Instead, I focused on the positive. Cassie was still responding and willing to make plans.

Joshua: Saturday is perfect. 6 p.m. at my place? I can send you the address.

She replied with a smile emoji.

That should have been the end of it. I should have put my phone away and finished my morning routine. But I couldn't do that when I had five pictures of Cassie barely covered in pink lace at my disposal.

Against my better judgment, I pulled the pictures back up. They looked like they were taken in front of a full-length mirror. I needed to buy one for my room. Then I could take her from behind while we face the mirror. Having a clear view of Cassie's face while I buried myself in her from that position was my new goal in life. My cock was straining in my pants just from the thought of it.

In the third picture, Cassie was leaning back against a bed while kneeling on the ground with her thighs spread apart. She was open and ready for me. God, I wished I knew what face she was making when she took the picture. I bet those blue eyes were drowning in lust as she thought about posing for me. That thought shouldn't get me so damn excited, but I couldn't stop myself from pulling out my dick.

I worked my shaft slowly, savoring the pleasure as I took in all the little details. One of Cassie's hands was holding her phone while the other was beneath the fabric of her panties. She probably touched herself until she climaxed.

My strokes grew quicker as I dove further into my fantasy, not once taking my eyes off of her. Cassie wanted me to look at her. That's why she sent me the pictures. I felt compelled to obey my naughty Goddess even when she wasn't actually around.

The empty room filled with grunts and moans as I stroked closer to completion. I could feel myself on the edge, ready to leap over at any moment. I conjured up the memory of Cassie in Florida and the way she sounded when she commanded me to come. That was all it took to send my body into a shuddering climax of pleasure.

"God fucking dammit," I vented my frustrations. A lovely mess of semen mocked me from the floor. I had been so in the moment that I forgot I was just standing in the middle of the damn kitchen. At least the tile made for an easy cleanup.

With the kitchen cleaned, I glanced at the clock. I was supposed to have left ten minutes ago if I didn't want to risk being late. Maybe I would be lucky and there wouldn't be a line for coffee.

Episode 10
Lost in a Dream

Cassie

The last one to class, all eyes were on me as I casually entered the room. With my head held high, I pretended not to notice everyone's silence over the disruption my entrance caused. The dramatics were totally on purpose. I was still embarrassed that I waited by my phone for so long last night and I blamed him. Acting out just a little for attention seemed like a great idea.

Power coursed through my veins as I caught Professor Grant tracking me out of the corner of my eye. I didn't acknowledge him or look his way. This was about my ability to grab his attention. Much like the lingerie pictures I sent earlier, I was presenting myself to him in a situation where he couldn't touch me. I wanted the professor to squirm with the agony of unfulfilled lust.

I fought the urge to clench my thighs. The little game was having an effect on me as well. Knowing that Professor Grant was watching me with the whole class around made me hot with desire.

Due to the small class size, everyone was seated towards the front. Only one in the group was vacant, and of course, it was next to

Jonathan. He gave me a wink and waved me over. *Great.* I could have sat somewhere else, but it would have been too awkward to sit away from everyone. Reluctantly, I took my seat with my smile frozen in place.

Once settled, I looked up and caught Professor Grant still staring. There was a flash of frustration when our eyes locked, but it disappeared the moment he looked away. I felt my confidence falter, confused by his reaction. I had been expecting lustful longing, not whatever that just was.

"I was worried for a moment you wouldn't show," Jonathan leaned over and whispered. He was all smiles as he invaded my personal bubble.

The hairs on the back of my neck prickled at the intrusion. Jonathan reminded me of every clueless guy who thought my space came with an open invitation for them. The intrusion was not welcome, but I didn't know how to convey that without causing a scene.

"I'm sure you would have been just fine if I hadn't." I teased Jonathan with a fake smile.

A mild dread seeped inside me as I realized how massive of a mistake it was to invite him bowling. Now my Friday night would be filled with the eager Jonathan integrating himself into my social circle. There would be no escape.

Professor Grant cleared his throat, pulling the class's attention to the front of the room. Irritation flashed over his features once more as he narrowed his gaze at Jonathan. Only Jonathan. The professor was jealous.

Taking the hint, Jonathan corrected his posture, removing him from my space in the process. Professor Grant's expression softened as he stole another glance in my direction. He just couldn't help himself, could he? We were going to have a long conversation about that later. I could not risk either academic or social scandals.

Seemingly pleased to have our attention, Professor Grant grabbed a stack of papers off his desk. He casually leaned against it and surveyed the class before speaking. I took the opportunity to do the same and noticed something I hadn't before. The four other girls in class each had laser sharp focus on the professor as they pe. rsued him with their lustful gazes.

Wishful thinking, bitches. Professor Grant is mine.

"I just want to start off by saying everyone did a decent job on their first paper. It will be interesting to see how everyone improves over the semester. The one thing I noticed most of you struggled with was setting the scene. You want the reader to lose themselves in the world you create. Too much detail can be just as bad as too little."

Professor Grant's voice was commanding but not abrasive as he droned on about grading our first assignment. The words were a formless blur melting into the background as I became distracted watching the professor. The way his arms moved fluidly as he spoke, accenting his point with various gestures, was more of a performance than a lecture. It made keeping focus on the words nearly impossible.

At some point, I lost track of what was going on in class. My mind was too busy conjuring the image of Professor Grant moaning my name while I teased him with my mouth. I wanted to explore his body at a leisurely pace while he slowly came undone.

Pay attention, Cassie!

"I'm going to hand back your papers now. It is in your best interest to read over my notes and put them to practice on your next paper," Professor Grant advised.

My heart sank as the professor walked around the room, returning everyone's papers. I spent the whole class zoned out with no idea what the next writing prompt was or when it was due. I was so wrapped up in my disappointment that I didn't notice when Professor Grant dropped off my paper.

"Print out your rough drafts and bring them in on Monday with a red pen. You will want them double spaced, trust me," Professor Grant chuckled. Well, one question was answered.

Everyone rose from their seats and vacated the classroom. Even Professor Grant seemed in a rush to leave. I felt sluggish and chastised myself as I gathered my things. Next week I would need to do better. Too much was at stake.

"So what if he is into you, Cass? Is he not your type?" Nicole dipped a french fry in ketchup, then lifted it to her lips as she awaited my answer.

"He's the old Cassie's type, which I am trying to get away from. Remember?" I rolled my eyes.

The conversation was killing my appetite. The poor bacon double cheeseburger sat on the plate before me, only half eaten. What a waste of mouth-watering ground beef.

Nicole had been sweet enough to grab burgers for the both of us. I had chosen my Jonathan dilemma as the first topic of our dinner conversation. It was a decision I was regretting heavily.

"You can't exactly control the kind of guy that turns you on, but you can control what you do with them," she explained with a wink and a smile.

I loved Nicole, but she was more of a one-night stand kind of gal. It gave her a wealth of knowledge on picking up men, but useless for relationship advice.

The conversation had been going in circles for a while now. While Nicole promised to be a buffer on Friday, she could not grasp why I wouldn't give Jonathan a test drive. She refused to admit it would make things awkward in class.

There was also the issue that I was now off the market, but Nicole didn't know that. To get her on the same page, I would have to open up a little about Professor Grant. My stomach twisted at the thought of spilling my secret.

"I have a confession," I announced with my eyes cast down. "I can't tell you much, yet. So please don't ask a lot of questions."

Clenched fists, my nails dug into my palms. I felt like a naughty child who was caught with their hand in the cookie jar. This was Nicole, my best friend. She wouldn't care. In fact, she would probably give me a high five.

Looking up, I saw Nicole's bright green eyes narrowed in my direction as she leaned over the table. "Why do I get the feeling I won't like this confession, Cassie?"

"I'm kind of involved with someone. He is exactly what I am looking for, but I need to keep him a secret." I was definitely the kid with her hand in the cookie jar.

"Why, Cassie?" Nicole asked. She had the look of a mother hen ready to peck someone's eyes out.

"He's handsome, and he lets me take control. Like really take control, Nicole—"

"Cassie!" Nicole snapped, causing me to flinch. She wasn't going to let this go without details. I didn't blame her.

"He is older. Like way older," I blurted. It wasn't the reason, but I couldn't tell her the whole truth.

Nicole blew out a breath as she sat back in her chair. The bewildered look on her face said more than her words. "Fuck, girl. Your grandmother would have an absolute fit.".

If she only knew.

"Exactly. It isn't that I am trying to hide anything from you, but the fewer people who know, the better. Especially since this is all very new." I gave my friend a pleading look. Nicole needed to be on my side.

"Fair enough. I won't push for details for now," Nicole said. The skepticism was painted all over her face. "We shouldn't tell Grace either. She has hang-ups about older men."

"Thanks for understanding."

Episode 11
Another Mess to Clean

Joshua

When did dating become so difficult? Or was it because whatever Cassie and I agreed to wasn't dating that made it so difficult? I knew we were exclusive. At least, that is what I took away from our meeting. No one else could touch her, only me. That was the agreement we made, and I had no reason to not believe her.

Except... she and Jonathan were openly flirting in front of the entire class. She warned me of that behavior if I wasn't good. Was that more punishment because I couldn't read her damn mind? If so, then we really needed that conversation about communication. I could play her little game if it made her smile, but the rules needed to be clear.

My hand tightened around my phone as I paced through the apartment. There was a slight tingle in my fingers as they went numb. If I could just talk to Cassie, I could relax. She would bring me back from the edge.

I tried to take a calming breath, but Jonathan's face flashed in my mind again. That jackass winked at her like he was picking up chicks at a bar. Then Cassie smiled at him. *My Cassie*. She shouldn't be smiling at other men, especially not that little prick.

I had been looking forward to seeing Cassie in class, but their little moment had threatened to sour my mood. I was incredibly close to making up some excuse to cut class short so I could avoid the torture of watching them together.

But then, my sweet Cassie turned her attention to me and Jonathan didn't get a second glance. He noticed too. There was nothing subtle about the way he kept glancing at her, or the look of defeat when he realized she would not look his way. Serves him right.

In a complete one-eighty from Monday's class, Cassie kept her precious blue eyes locked on me. She seemed utterly entranced by my every move. I didn't feel nervous or uncomfortable like when the other girls watched me with their dreamy expressions. Because it was Cassie, it was okay.

With a group that small, I would normally try to engage them more during class, but the idea of breaking whatever spell Cassie was under stopped me. The only thing that mattered was keeping that dreamy look on her face as she watched me. To my credit, I gave a damn good impromptu lecture. At the end of the day, it was a harmless indulgence. Plenty of professors exclusively lectured. It wasn't like anyone's education was being impaired.

A long sigh escaped me as I looked back down at my phone. I missed the sound of her voice and the way she said *good boy*. Just thinking about it sent a shiver down my spine. Calling her shouldn't be so hard, but I had spent the last hour stalling.

"You are forty years old, not sixteen. Just fucking call her," I scolded myself.

To combat the loneliness, I had resorted to talking to myself out loud more and more since returning from Florida.

Being alone had never bothered me in the past. Janet and I rarely spent time apart aside from work. I never wanted to bore her by making her just sit and watch me grade papers, and those tasks were always so time-consuming that I never noticed I was alone.

After the breakup, I was barely on my own before Eddie insisted on a summer vacation. He kept me busy, rarely leaving me to my own devices. As nice as it was, it left me completely unprepared for my new life of solitude.

Then again, all the preparation in the world wouldn't have made a damn bit of difference once I met Cassie. Thoughts of her consumed me in the quiet moments, which were a frequent occurrence now. I couldn't be alone because I wanted her. No, I needed her.

Determined not to become any more pathetic, I unlocked the screen and scrolled through my contacts until I found Goddess. A smile crossed my lips at the name. She was a goddess, my goddess. My thumb hovered over the contact for a second before pressing the call button.

Panic sparked as soon as I dialed. What if she didn't pick up? Would I just leave a message? I had no idea what I would even say.

"Hello, Cassie. You were upset I didn't call last night, so I am calling now. Please tell me I am a good boy!" Nope. Nope. I couldn't say that.

Struggling to breathe, I held the phone to my ear and listened to it ring. Each second I waited sank me further into doubt. If she didn't pick up, I was going to have a panic attack.

Pick up. My palms were slick with sweat. *Pick up.* I should have texted first. *Pick up.* Do they even talk on the phone anymore or is it all texting? *Please, pick up!*

"Hello, Joshua," her sultry voice greeted me. My name had never sounded more beautiful. It evoked images of Cassie riding me and chasing her pleasure with my body while she chanted my name over and over.

And just like that, my anxiety was gone. Cassie's brightness melted all of it away, and all she did was say my name.

"What happened to Professor Grant?" I teased.

"My roommate is home. I don't think she can hear me in my room, but you never know," she replied in a hushed voice.

"Yeah, that could be pretty bad," I agreed. It was another reminder from the universe that I shouldn't be doing this. Fuck off, universe. I would not back down now.

"If you don't want me calling you by your name, I could just call you *good boy*," she taunted. The magic words rolled off her tongue like a siren's call.

Fuck. My cock liked the sound of that. It began to stir, eager to respond to the goddess on the other end of the line.

"Call me anything you want. I just want to hear your sweet voice."

Her giggle in response made me long to see her smile. I wanted nothing more than to hold Cassie in my arms and kiss her delicate lips. If the situation were different, I would be in my car driving to her place to make it a reality. But Cassie was my student, and she had a roommate making it impossible.

"You like listening to me talk?" she asked, almost innocently. I couldn't tell if she was baiting me or was genuinely surprised.

"I like a lot of things about you, Cassie," I replied.

"Is that so? You don't even know me that well. A little presump-tuous, don't you think?" There was no bite to her challenge. It was nothing more than playful banter to provoke a reaction. If Cassie wanted to play, then who was I to deny her?

"I know the sounds you make when you lose yourself to pleasure. I know the taste of your delicious cunt. And I know pink is an excellent color on you. All of those things I like about you. I could go on if you'd like." The words flowed easily as I rediscovered my charm.

The voice in the back of my head was cautioning me not to be so forward, but I ignored it easily enough. My body was awake and starving for Cassie. I was going to indulge myself with her one way or another.

"Oh," Cassie said, her voice a mix of arousal and surprise. "What about my writing?"

The question caught me a tad off guard. Of course, I had enjoyed her paper, repeatedly, but I also graded it and left notes as if it were a normal assignment so I had something to hand back. Was Cassie under the impression I didn't like it because of that?

I kept my voice level, determined not to convey my worry. "The paper you turned in? It caught me off guard at first, but I couldn't put it down. I lost count of how many times I read it."

That was a lie. I read the thing five times since it was turned in and pleasured myself three of those times. I went as far as to scan the stupid thing and load it onto a thumb drive so I could read it some more after I returned the original.

"I figured by the mess you left," Cassie said, amused. She noticed the cum stain from my first read-through. *Great job, Joshua.*

"I, um, sorry about that. I may have gotten a little too excited at one point," I confessed sheepishly. "I can't control myself when I think of you."

"Do you think of me and touch yourself a lot?" Cassie asked in a low, lustful voice.

She sounded as turned on as I felt, and it drove me wild. I reached down with my free hand and started rubbing my erection over my pants, desperate for stimulation.

"All the fucking time," I admitted without even thinking. Cassie was my truth serum. She could ask me anything and I would tell her.

"Really? When was the last time?" I could hear the pleasure in her question. The naughty little thing liked me stroking myself to thoughts of her.

"This morning. I couldn't help myself after you sent those pictures. Pink really is your color." My voice was rough with need as I continued to palm my dick through the fabric.

"Maybe I should make it a habit of snapping a few pics before I get dressed every morning if you don't think it will be too distracting the days we have class together."

My brain short-circuited as I processed her words. Was Cassie suggesting—

"You actually wore that today?" I blurted out in surprise.

There was not much to the lingerie in those pictures. They were definitely not everyday wear, and yet Cassie had worn them to class. She sat in front of me wearing naughty pink lace under her clothes. I tried to swallow, but my mouth was dry.

"Um, yeah. Did you think I did a whole photo shoot before class and then changed?" Cassie laughed.

I didn't even care. Let her laugh. My thoughts were still trying to piece everything together. I had assumed that maybe she took them the night before. Never in my wildest dreams would I have guessed that she would wear so little under her clothes.

The pictures from the morning flashed through my mind repeatedly. The way her body was on display for me and me alone. That thong was so miniscule even by a thong's standard. She may as well have been sitting in class with no panties at all.

"Fuck, Cassie," I moaned as I freed my cock from my pants. My little nymph had pushed me over the edge. "Are you still wearing them now?"

"Maybe. What if I am? Will you touch yourself for me?" she asked teasingly. She was definitely still wearing them.

A soft grunt escaped me in response as my hand leisurely began stroking up and down my shaft. I conjured the image of my Cassie sitting on the bed from the pictures, her bed, covered only in thin strips of pink lace. With one hand on her phone, the other was free to explore her body.

I bet she touched herself after, desperate to relieve the ache she felt for me.

"Joshua? I asked you a question." Cassie's words pulled me from my fantasy.

"I am right now," I answered quickly, eager to obey.

Precum beaded at my tip as I continued to work myself. My eyes fell shut as I pictured her pink lips pressed to the head of my cock. Her soft, warm tongue licked the tip clean.

"Such a good boy. How should I reward you?" Cassie cooed seductively.

I was a slave to those two words. They were a collar around my neck, holding me in submission to my mistress. I was hers to command without question.

As for my reward? That was simple.

"Please, my goddess, touch yourself for me. I need to hear you." I was practically begging my request.

The seconds ticked by as I waited. Soon, the familiar sounds of Cassie's pleasure danced around me. They were as exquisite as I remembered. The speed of my strokes quickened as her moans flamed my arousal into an inferno.

"You sound so beautiful, Cassie. Do you ever think of me and touch yourself? Tell me you do." The words were choked between moans.

"Yes," she replied breathlessly between moans. Such a simple word had my blood pounding and my cock aching to be buried inside her.

"But it is never enough to dull the ache, is it? My goddess needs *me* to worship her body and make her feel good."

"Tell me how," Cassie commanded. Her words tightened the invisible collar. My need to please her forced me into blissful submission.

"I would start on my knees. You like me on my knees, don't you?" My question was dark and hungry.

Sweet moans floated through the line, calling to me like a siren's song. It felt like too much and not enough all at the same time. The need to drive Cassie mad with lust spurred me to continue as I pumped myself closer to the edge.

"I would kiss your ankles, working my way up to your inner thighs. I would take my time so I can savor the feel of your skin. Then I would lick those pretty pink panties, teasing you until I can taste you through them. Imagine my tongue licking your delicious pussy until you are squirming on my face, begging me for more. How long could I lick you before you come? I wouldn't stop worshiping your sweet pussy until you completely fell apart."

I was panting heavily between words. The picture I painted for Cassie had me just as excited. The need to taste her again was driving me close to madness.

More precum beaded at the tip as I felt myself getting closer. This wouldn't do. I couldn't spill before she climaxed. Her pleasure had to come before mine. Reluctantly, I slowed my pace to try to hold off my orgasm.

"You are making me so wet, Joshua. I can slide my fingers in so easily." Cassie sounded like sex as she spoke, making my cock ache for her.

"The next time I see you, I am going to have you dripping for me, Cassie. Then I am going to fuck that pretty pussy with my thick cock until you come all over it, over and over. You are going to love feeling so stretched and full while I fuck you through your climax. I will not stop until you are a whimpering mess of orgasms. Come for me, Cassie. Show me what it will sound like." I was practically growling out the words.

"I'm coming! Oh, fuck! Joshua, I'm coming!" Cassie cried out the strangled words. Her voice squeaked through her moans as I listened to her ride out the orgasm until she was gasping for breath.

My climax followed, triggered by the intoxicating noises Cassie produced. I arched back, leaning against the hallway wall, as white ropes of cum sprayed forth. It felt like forever before my balls were empty.

"That was, um. You make me…" I struggled to find the words as I tried to catch my breath.

Cassie giggled, though I could hear the exhaustion in her voice. Her joy was infectious, and I found myself letting loose a small chuckle.

"I can't wait for Saturday. Are you absolutely sure you have plans tomorrow night?" I knew the answer, but that didn't stop me from trying. If there was even a sliver of a chance I could convince her to see me sooner, then I had to take it.

"Patience, Professor," she chided softly.

"What happened to being cautious because of your roommate?" I teased.

"Fuck. You jumbled my brain with all your sexy words. I need to go. Goodnight."

"Goodnight, my sweet Cassie."

The call ended, leaving me in a satisfied silence. All I had to do was survive one more day, and then I would have Cassie. This time would be perfect.

I took a step toward the bathroom, eager to get a washcloth to clean myself, when something moist and sticky seeped through my sock.

"Damn it," I muttered as I looked down. In my excitement, I hadn't paid a damn bit of attention and made a mess of the carpet and wall.

Shoulders slumped in defeat, I headed to the bathroom to clean myself. The mess in the hallway could wait until after.

Episode 12

Three is a Crowd

Joshua

The parking lot was packed at Pine Grove Lanes, which surprised no one. It was a Friday night in a college town, and the bowling alley was hosting some sort of drinking event. Booze and bowling with a bunch of college kids seemed like a disaster to me. How many bowling balls would I see flying through the air before the night was over? At least the event was twenty-one and up, so it probably wouldn't be that bad.

So, why would a less-than-enthused college professor spend his precious free time at an event crawling with students? In a single word, Eddie. I should have been grateful to have a best friend who cares enough about me he doesn't want me sitting at home alone moping on a Friday night. I wasn't, though. I was annoyed more than anything.

The original plan was to spend Friday night catching up on the ever-growing backlog of shows that I had let pile up. I had been so busy with the new semester and Cassie that I thought my brain could use a night off.

Eddie disagreed. He made it very clear he expected me to spend the evening wallowing in self-pity and loneliness while left to my own devices. He had every reason to believe that, because I hadn't told him about my new obsession. Rarely did I keep secrets from Eddie, but I hadn't figured out how to bring it up.

Hey, Eddie! Remember that hot blonde at the bar in Florida that you insisted was safe to fuck around with? Turns out she is my student this semester! Crazy, huh?

And now my mind was flooded with thoughts of her. Dammit.

I had been working not to think about Cassie this evening. Since our phone call last night, things had shifted between us. This morning, I was greeted by a new set of risqué pictures from her. My thank you texts evolved into a casual conversation that carried us through most of the day.

I longed to read over the messages again and ease some of the ache, but now was not the time. I couldn't risk Eddie or Carla innocently peeking over my shoulder. How would I explain myself without exposing my secret?

I hoped to be busy enough tonight that my mind wouldn't stray to her. The last thing I wanted to do was bother her when she made it clear she would be otherwise occupied, but now that the thought was there, it would not leave so easily.

My palms itched, eager to type a quick text to my goddess and let her know I was thinking of her, but I refrained. It hadn't even been a full two hours since our last conversation.

She had asked my opinion on heels, sending me a picture of her wearing a pair. To be honest, I was more interested in her long legs than the shoes. Leave it to Cassie to have me growing stiff over the thought of her legs.

I should have worn looser pants, dammit.

As discreetly as possible, I adjust myself so my excitement would be less obvious. Getting an erection in a place like this was not ideal. If I was home alone, then I would just take care of it. But I wasn't home or alone. I was stuck as a third wheel on another one of Eddie's *not-a-date dates* with Carla.

Nothing against Carla, but I was getting agitated being Eddie's security blanket every time he took her out. It was one thing when I was dating Janet. Then, it was more of a double date. Now, I was being dragged along, and I had no idea the reason why.

"Do you hate bowling that much, Josh?" Carla nudged me with a smile.

The tight curls of her brown hair bounced as she gave me another quick nudge. The last thing I wanted was for my craptastic mood to ruin the evening for Carla. It wasn't her fault Eddie kept dragging me along.

"No, I just don't enjoy mingling with students. This place is crawling with them," I explained with a sigh. It wasn't a complete lie. We were probably the oldest people here.

Why Eddie chose here, of all places, I couldn't figure out. Normally, I would make the trek closer to where Carla, Eddie, and Janet lived and worked in the next town over. The thirty-minute drive was a small price I gladly paid repeatedly for a night free of college students.

Typically, Eddie avoided the college scene as well. Drunken frat boys were something neither of us had the patience for anymore. He also knew the struggles I had with the female student body after listening to my woes over the years. Although he never seemed to take that particular issue seriously.

"Really?" Eddie cut in. "Because you dressed like you came to melt the girls' panties tonight." There was an edge to his voice I didn't recognize or like.

My knee-jerk reaction was to roll my eyes and say something snarky in return, but I held back. Starting a fight over my clothes would accomplish nothing and would have probably made Carla uncomfortable.

For the record, nothing about my clothes screamed panty melter. The white t-shirt, jeans, and leather jacket was a regular staple of mine when we went out. The very idea that I would be dressed to pick up girls knowing where we were going was an insult. I had no idea what suddenly crawled up my friend's ass, but I was not in the mood when he was the one who dragged me out.

"You haven't shaved in a few days, either. That isn't going to help keep the young ladies away. Unless you are hoping to find someone?" Carla teased.

Her delicate fingers reached up to scratch the scruff I had grown in the last two days to accentuate her point. I froze like a deer staring down the headlights of an oncoming vehicle. Her soft touch along my stubble felt nicer than I would ever admit, but it didn't matter. This would never, ever happen.

Even if I wasn't completely enamored by Cassie, Carla was not on my radar. She never had been and never would be. Eddie's interest in her was obvious before I even met her. The dreamy look in his eye every time he talked about her gave it away. Just because he was being an absolute idiot dragging his feet didn't mean I would ignore the obvious feelings he had for her. For better or worse, Eddie was my best friend.

I had hoped that Eddie would rescue me from my rather uncomfortable predicament. Unfortunately, my silent panicked plea was met with his icy glare of jealousy. By the time I finally stepped back, Eddie was already stomping his way inside the bowling alley.

I let out a frustrated sigh as my shoulders slumped in defeat. Tonight seemed destined for disaster. If I wanted to salvage it, then I would have to set boundaries.

"Listen, Carla—"

"Bob in accounting asked me out on a date," she interrupted me.

The declaration left me confused. I stood there with my mouth gaping like a fish while I tried to figure out why she was telling me.

When I finally spoke, the words came out a bit flustered. "Okay? Um, congrats? I'm sorry that's just so random, but Bob? In accounting? Really, Carla? That sounds made up." Her flat expression threatened to crack when I followed up with a smile and a wink.

"Yes. Bob in accounting. He is nice and cute. I was going to say yes, but Eddie insisted he was taking me out instead," Carla explained as I nodded along. "He said he was taking me bowling."

My best friend was a bigger idiot than I gave him credit for. There was no way this was a miscommunication. Either Eddie asked Carla on a date and then invited me along, or he purposely misled her. It was a little surprising she had kept up the smiles until now.

"I am sorry, Carla. Not that it makes it any better, but I was brought against my will." I shouldn't have been the one apologizing, but the culprit was conveniently inside throwing an unearned tantrum. Guilty by association.

"That makes it worse," she replied flatly, her arms crossed.

"Yes, it does," I agreed.

Another silence fell between us as I took in a deep breath. This was not my mess to fix.

But...

He was my oldest friend and usually loyal to a fault. During the darkest moments with Janet, he had my back. As shitty as the situation was, nothing good would come from throwing him under the bus. If anything, it would just exacerbate things.

"I get you're mad, I really do, but flirting with me isn't going to get you anywhere with Eddie. I think you know that," I said as I nudged her shoulder with mine.

Carla let out a small sigh as she looked towards the entrance. "I do, and I'm sorry to drag you in the middle of it."

"Technically, Eddie dragged me in the middle of it when he invited me," I replied with a grin.

The corners of Carla's lips curled into a small smile. Her body shook ever so slightly with a chuckle that she was trying to suppress. There was still hope this night could turn around. At least things couldn't get much worse with Carla and me on the same page about Eddie.

Having decided our little conversation was over, she grabbed my hand and led me inside the bowling alley.

Stepping inside the bowling alley was like traveling back in time. Black lights illuminated the space, giving everything around us a faint purple glow. My white tee was especially bright. I shifted uncomfortably as I realized a little too late that it was a bright billboard for unwanted attention. The only saving grace was the number of other bowlers who seemed to be glowing unintentionally as well.

The pop music drifting over the crowd was loud enough to hear but soft enough not to overpower conversations. The scene took me back to the late-night cosmic bowling events of my teens. My friends and I frequented them in our childhood, but not so much as we got older. The whole thing seemed a bit juvenile for college kids, but everyone was laughing and having a good time. Maybe it was the alcohol.

"Oh my God!" Carla squealed over the music. "I loved the whole black light bowling thing growing up!" Her joyful admission was yet another reminder that I didn't belong here. Eddie should have been the one watching her eyes sparkle with delight. Granted, he was the one who stomped away like a toddler, but if I had not been here...

My internal pity party broke when a feminine voice catcalled a familiar nickname. "Hey there, Professor Hottie!"

My posture straightened as the hairs on the back of my neck bristled. I should have pretended I didn't hear them, but it was too late. The gaggle of giggles not far from where we stood told me they saw my reaction. *Fuck me.*

A familiar nauseous feeling spread through me as I tried to mask my discomfort. This was why I didn't venture to these kinds of places. The students knew better on campus, but social events with alcohol were different. The girls became bolder after a few drinks lowered their inhibitions. No one ever seemed to care how it affected me.

You would think after all this time I would be used to the leering and catcalls. You would think the attention of younger women would be flattering. It wasn't. It never felt good when it came from a random student. Between the disrespect for my position and the worry that I could lose my job, it created stress.

Carla looked up at me with confusion that slowly morphed to sympathy as she realized who the girls were shouting at. My shoulders slumped in defeat as I waited for the response that I knew was coming. Sure enough, her brow pulled together in concern as she mouthed the word *sorry*.

Pity. I hated that response almost as much as the catcalls and notes. The way Carla looked at me, as if she knew how powerless I felt in the moment, was humiliating. I was a grown man, dammit!

That was the final straw. The nail in the coffin. I. Was. Done.

I made my way through the crowd toward Eddie at the shoe counter. My intentions were to calmly, but firmly, explain to my friend that he needed to get his head out of his ass. I was not going to put up with all of this garbage just because he was afraid to be alone with his crush. I was going home.

Both Eddie and the poor pimple-faced teen behind the counter flinched when I approached and forcefully slammed my palm on the counter. *Shit, that was a bit more dramatic than intended*. I opened my mouth, ready to deliver the speech I carefully crafted on my way over, only to lose all focus.

A familiar voice carried across the room, cutting through all the other noise. The heavenly laughter took hold of me, calling me to her like a siren on the rocks among the waves. My head turned towards the melodious giggles, and I saw her.

Cassie.

The entire world melted away as I watched her laughing with a group of her peers. My brain barely registered the others around her. The only thing that mattered was Cassie. She was stunning in a shimmering tank top and jeans so tight that they looked painted on. A beautiful goddess fit to be worshiped.

My cock was especially appreciative of those jeans and the way they hugged her perfect ass. It stiffened as my body begged me to march over there and *appreciate* the woman who owned me thoroughly.

"Josh?" Eddie called my name, waving a hand in front of my face. "Everything okay?"

Yes. No. Maybe? I had no idea how to answer that question. Now was not the time to confess about Cassie and my transgressions, nor the plethora of lewd thoughts suddenly running through my mind. Instead of diving headfirst into the beautiful clusterfuck that my life had become this past week, I simply nodded.

Eddie studied me as I struggled to keep my eyes off Cassie. We both knew I was lying, but only I knew why. I silently prayed he would not pry the answer out of me in such a crowded place.

"Are you sure?" he pressed. Suspicion clouded his features as he leaned closer. "It isn't like you to space out randomly. What is going on?"

My body tensed as dread slowly trickled through me. If Eddie saw Cassie, he might recognize her. Then again, maybe he wouldn't. She looked a little different dolled-up, and he never saw her up close that night.

My thoughts continued to swirl, fueling my panic. I was speechless while Eddie continued to study me. My hands clenched into fists as I tried to steady myself. I was seconds away from jumping out of my own skin.

Please, God, give me a distraction. Any distraction.

"Kiss and make-up yet, boys? Or is Eddie still pouting?" Carla teased us as she rejoined the group.

Eddie immediately shifted his focus and his eyes shamelessly roamed up and down her body for the umpteenth time this evening. He was fooling no one.

Thrilled to no longer be the center of attention, I relaxed a little. A second longer and I might have cracked under the pressure.

Eddie maneuvered himself around me so he could stand closer to Carla. He was a hunter, and she was his prey.

"First of all, I wasn't pouting," Eddie insisted as he playfully poked at her shoulder. Carla waved him off dismissively before scrunching her nose and smiling.

Their little back and forth filled me with envy. Eddie had no idea how lucky he was that he could pursue the object of his desires so openly. And what did he do with the privilege? He squandered it time and time again.

Was I frustrated because Eddie was finally flirting with Carla or because he was doing such a piss-poor job?

With the two distracted by each other, I stole another glance in Cassie's direction. My peek was timed perfectly as it was her turn to bowl. I watched as she bent over, those tight jeans hugging her ass, to release the ball down the lane. Her movements were fluid, as if my goddess knew I was watching and wanted to show off. It was all too much to take. I had to look away before I did something foolish.

Carla and Eddie seemed to have settled down, so we gathered our shoes from the pimple-faced kid. Eddie had the forethought to reserve us a lane in advance. It made me curious if this little excursion was as last minute as he originally claimed or something he had in the works for a while. I followed quietly as he led us to our spot.

Nerves took hold as we passed Cassie's lane. It was a strange mix of longing and fear. I wanted her to notice me despite the complications it might cause. Just the thought of my name on her lips made my cock twitch.

"Holy shit! Professor Grant?" a familiar male voice called out.

Episode 13

Back Alley Dealings

Joshua

I barely fought back a shudder as I stopped and turned toward the young man who had become the villain in my story. Was I being childish? Maybe.

"Hello, Jonathan," I greeted with a tight smile. It was physically painful to be pleasant to him.

"I wasn't expecting to see any professors here," he said with a nervous laugh.

The way he stood there expectantly, like we should engage in conversation, caught me off guard. It took me a moment to realize why he would even say hello.

Fuck me, please don't be one of those little ass kissers.

Occasionally, students would try to befriend me. It was always awkward and unwelcome. Unlike the flirtatious ones, these types were bolder from the beginning as they blatantly overstepped boundaries in their misguided attempts to become friends.

I stood there with an unamused expression and let the uncomfortable silence between us grow. Some chattering behind Jonathan caught my attention. Cassie's blue eyes locked with mine, and I realized just how fucked I was.

My sweet goddess captured my attention so completely before that I had not noticed anyone else in her group. Jonathan was here with Cassie. Once again, he was trying to encroach on my territory. Jealousy surged through my veins like poison that threatened to destroy me.

My eyes narrowed as they locked with Jonathan's. I held back the small smile that wanted to break free as I watched him fidget nervously under my gaze. This quiet had only lasted ten seconds, at most, but it was more than long enough to assert my dominance.

"Professors are people, Jonathan. Am I not allowed a life outside of my job? Is it written somewhere that I can't go bowling?" My tone was cold and flat, my teacher's voice. It was something I rarely used because of how demeaning it was to the other person, but that was the point. I wanted to intimidate him and break him down with Cassie watching.

"O-of course not. Sorry, Professor Grant. I didn't mean..." Jonathan stumbled over his words, clearly stressed by our interaction.

Satisfied with my little display, I looked back at Cassie and gave her a small smile. "Have fun, you two. See you both in class on Monday."

I turned and walked off before she could respond. Rude? Maybe, but I had to put some distance between us even if it drove me insane. If I had stayed there any longer, I would have punched Jonathan before dragging Cassie away.

"What was that about?" Carla asked as I rejoined my little group.

"Nothing," I said as I shook my head, "just some students saying hello."

Eddie shot me a sympathetic look as if he finally realized the situation he created. He took a step forward, looking at me as if he wanted to discuss it further, but I raised my hand in protest. I was already here, an apology or check-in would not change that.

The evening dragged slower than a snail. *Is that even an expression?* I was stuck watching Eddie flirt with Carla with an intensity I had never seen before. No doubt her little act earlier lit a fire under him. I would have been happier for them if I didn't have to sit front row at the event.

At some point, I stopped bowling and focused more on the beer and nachos. Carla tried to keep me in the conversation every so often and I indulged her efforts, but being ignored was better.

Every so often, I would steal a look in Cassie's direction. It was a special kind of torture watching her with her friends, knowing I couldn't join them. Not now and not in the future.

I tried to convince myself that it was okay because she was having a good time, except I wasn't so sure that she was. More than once I caught her trying to outmaneuver Jonathan's attempts to touch her. It made my blood boil every single time.

My breaking point was when Cassie bowled a strike. Her entire group was cheering so loud in celebration that it caught the attention of the entire establishment. When Jonathan picked her up and spun her around, I had finally had enough.

The commotion was a big enough distraction that no one noticed as I slipped away.

Past the restrooms was a rear exit that led to the alley. Soaking in the cool night air as I stepped outside, the quiet darkness helped a calmness settle over me as I found space to breathe for the first time that night.

This shouldn't have been as hard as it was. I had spent most of the day texting with Cassie. She was coming over to my place tomorrow night. I just needed to be patient.

Or call the whole thing off...

No, that was not an option. Cassie was in charge, and I couldn't see her just letting me go. Even if she did, it wasn't what I truly wanted. The pain and frustration were making me crazy, but not having her would drive me over the edge.

I leaned against the brick wall and closed my eyes. Lost in my thoughts, I didn't notice the door creak open as someone else joined me outside.

"Here you are. I thought maybe you left," a soft voice broke through the silence. I jumped to attention, startled and embarrassed to be caught like this by *her*.

"Cassie. Why aren't you inside with Jonathan and the others?" I questioned. The way her face scrunched in disgust when I said his name made me happier than it should have.

"You disappeared. I was curious where you went... and if you were alone," she confessed.

The pause mid-sentence gave me a little chuckle. There was something amusing about my sweet goddess being jealous. She hadn't figured out yet that she consumed my every waking thought and desire. All I wanted was her.

Cassie shot me a look that warned she wasn't as amused as I was. That sobered me up real quick.

I straightened my posture as she approached me with hungry eyes. Her palm applied soft pressure to my chest as she pushed me firmly against the wall. Once she had me braced, her touch roamed down my body with purpose until she was rubbing my dick to life through my jeans.

"Fuck. Cassie," I moaned blissfully. My eyes fell shut as I reached out to touch her while I ground my growing erection into her hand. She could make me cum in my pants, and I would eagerly thank her for it.

"Hands against the wall," Cassie ordered.

My body obeyed without hesitation or conscious thought. At some point, I subconsciously made peace with my role in this. I was nothing more than the demands of my goddess, and it felt freeing.

The rough texture of the brick scratched at my palms as I pressed them into the wall. The sensation was a strange contrast to the pleasure Cassie was administering. It amplified the experience in a way.

"Such a good boy," she praised. "You like it when I play with you, don't you, Professor Grant?"

"Yes, my goddess," I agreed as my head rested against the wall.

"Be good and don't move without permission." Her sultry voice danced around me as she gave the order.

Suddenly, Cassie dropped to her knees in front of me. Confused, I reached out to pull her off the dirty ground, but swiftly stopped myself as I remembered her command. I quickly pressed myself flat against the wall and hoped she hadn't noticed.

My goddess was stunning on her knees. I watched in awe as she unfastened my jeans and eagerly freed my throbbing erection. My cock wept with precum in anticipation of all that was to come.

Cassie was touching me in ways she had not before. Her hands explored my length with a hunger that had me ready to explode all over her. That thought alone sent me spiraling as images of her painted white with my release danced through my mind. I closed my eyes and took a few measured breaths as I desperately tried to calm myself.

She is only holding your cock, Joshua. Plenty of women have had their hands on it.

But none of them were Cassie.

When I opened my eyes, I was greeted with the sight of her lips a hair's breadth away from my cock. I could have easily grabbed those beautiful blonde locks in a fist and fucked that little mouth of hers until my cum was pouring down her throat. It was so tempting, but I had been ordered not to move. The need to please her was far greater than my need for release. For now.

"This is mine," she said and gave the tip a quick lick. I groaned in both ecstasy and frustration. I needed more, so much more. "I want to make sure you remember who it belongs to. I don't like people playing with my toys without permission."

"All yours," I agreed, barely hanging on.

Truthfully, I had no idea what I had agreed to. I was far too lost in how amazing her tongue felt. My body was humming with pleasure after such a small taste. I would have said anything if it meant she would keep going.

"That's right, *professor*." The last word sounded absolutely filthy as it fell from her lips. Never had I enjoyed a woman calling me that... until Cassie.

This woman has turned my world on its head. I had never submitted to any woman before. It never even occurred to me. Being in charge, dominating my partner, and having all the control, always felt so natural. Roles were never discussed and agreed upon. It was just how things happened. I would have never imagined myself in this situation in a million years—my body pressed against the wall while Cassie slowly teased me to death.

My body was tense as I fought to remain still. Every muscle burned from the strain of holding back. The pain kept me from completely losing myself and ravishing her on the ground.

"Cassie, please. I can't—" I could barely choke out my plea.

"You can and you will," she replied all too quickly.

This was nothing more than a game to her. For some strange reason, that made my torture even more exquisite. I was going to die like this, and I no longer cared.

Everything blurred when her lips wrapped around my cock, finally giving me relief. My fingers dug into the wall behind me as the pain continued to keep me grounded. I could no longer think. My mind was consumed with the feel of Cassie's tongue stroking my cock while she sucked me off.

My incoherent ramblings of pleasure echoed through the empty alley. I should have been worried someone might come to investigate the noise, but I wasn't. Such thoughts were beyond me. The only thing that mattered was the pressure building as I inched closer to my orgasm.

I was close, so very close. A familiar tightness in my balls signaled I was right on the edge.

Right before my orgasm could take hold and grant me the euphoric release that I so desperately needed, Cassie pulled away. I stared in utter disbelief as she stood up and dusted the dirt from her pants.

"I'm sorry," I blurted out. It was the only logical thing to say. I must have done something wrong. Why else would she just stop?

"For?" She stared back at me, looking as confused as I felt.

"I-I don't know? If you aren't mad, then why did you stop?" My head was still spinning from being so close. My cock ached with a pain I never thought possible.

Cassie laughed in response. I watched her eyes sparkle, lost as to what about this situation was so damn humorous.

"I stopped because I didn't want to risk the mess," she explained. Apparently, Cassie had never heard of swallowing.

"That was just cruel," I complained.

"Yet you would let me do it to you again and again and again, wouldn't you, *professor*?" She used that sexy vixen voice again, the one that made me bend to her will in an instant.

I looked away, frustrated that Cassie was right. More right than she probably realized. I would gladly reenact every moment if she asked. Did that make me pathetic?

When I didn't make a move to pull up my pants, Cassie moved to redress me. I stood there and let her while I tried to make sense of it all.

"You are still coming over tomorrow, I hope?" I hated how small I sounded, but there was still the fear that this was some sort of punishment. If something was wrong, then I needed her to be honest so I could fix it.

"Hey," Cassie said as she tilted my face towards her, "stop getting so inside your own head. I don't like when you do that."

Before I could object, my darling goddess pressed her lips to mine and kissed me. It wasn't passionate or intense. There were no fireworks or sparks. This was somehow more. It was a comforting gesture that melted away all my fears and frustrations. When the kiss ended, I was much calmer.

"Thank you," I whispered as our lips parted. This girl was truly amazing. She seemed to know exactly what I needed, even when I did not.

"Well, I need to get back inside before Nicole sends a search party. See you tomorrow, Professor Grant." Cassie bid me farewell and headed back inside.

I stayed outside for a bit longer as I tried to fully understand what was happening. How could she have ingrained herself so far under my skin in such a short time? Every single interaction was like a roller coaster with all the ups and downs.

I would say I was falling for Cassie, but that wasn't true. It couldn't be. We still barely knew each other. This was nothing more than unbridled lust. I was merely chasing the high and nothing more.

Episode 14

First World Problems

Cassie

"How was the first week of classes, dear?" my grandmother asked with faux interest as she cut off a piece from the strip of bacon on her plate.

The elderly woman sat across from me dressed in her traditional brunch attire with the same fake smile she always wore in public. Her green Chanel suit reminded me of that pink number Marge Simpson wore in that one episode. If grandmother knew her outfit resembled a bargain buy outfit from a cartoon, she would lose her mind.

That would make brunch interesting for a change.

"Pretty good, actually," I replied with a smile.

My mind was only half in the conversation. The sound of her knife and fork as it scraped against her plate screeched as she cut off another small piece of bacon. Only Agnes Ainsworth would be too snobbish to touch bacon with her bare hands. It was embarrassing.

"Do any of your professors know who you are yet?" Aunt Margaret inquired from the seat next to me.

"Of course they do, Margaret," Grandmother answered before I could. "It is her third year. Every staff member should be well aware of who Cassidy is."

I didn't bother to correct her. If Agnes Ainsworth knew just how wrong she was, she would march onto campus and make a scene in the dean's office. The bitch was all about name recognition and status. She would be livid if she knew the lengths I went to in order to distance myself from the Ainsworth name.

The Ainsworth family has donated countless sums of money to the university over the decades. The campus even had a few buildings with the Ainsworth name plastered on them, one of the more obvious marks of her influence. There was also the scholarship program and the benefits. It all inflated her ego and gave her the false impression she alone owned PGU.

It was a small comfort that my last name was Jones. It gave me a chance to make first impressions that weren't influenced by my family. I could never predict how the professors would react when they finally discovered the connection. Some would try to suck up to me, hoping to earn my favor and, in turn, more funding for their departments. Others would become merciless with the assumption I needed a reality check because everything must have been handed to me in life. Rarely was I treated the same once the truth came out.

Aunt Margaret gave me a sympathetic look. Broaching the topic in front of Grandmother had been a mistake, no doubt. I have made similar mistakes in the past, like accidentally referring to her as "Aunt Mags" in front of Grandmother. The lecture for my *insolence* was bizarre and demeaning. I have been overly cautious when dealing with the bitch ever since.

Aunt Margaret changed the subject quickly to a random topic that didn't involve me. I was grateful for the deflection even if it was only needed because of her slip-up. My aunt was the champ at wrangling her mother. Minor slips were easy to forgive since she often acted as the protector who shielded me from the old lady's bullshit.

I let them drone on without me while I pushed the food around on my plate. The meal was the only reason I still joined every Saturday, but my heart wasn't in it today. The talk of school made me think of Professor Grant.

Last night in the alley, I had surprised myself. Giving blow jobs behind bowling alleys was not something I did. Most guys were so needy that it always felt more like a chore.

Professor Grant was different. I had expected him to push the issue when I stopped before he could finish, but instead he apologized. The entire exchange threw me off balance.

If I was being honest with myself, I was initially disappointed with the lack of confrontation. I wanted to fight, assert myself, and regain the control that stayed just out of reach the entire evening.

Up until that point, I had been spiraling. Jonathan took every opportunity to softly push at my boundaries by testing repeatedly for an opening. I felt uncomfortable being direct when surrounded by so many people, which only made him bolder with his advances.

By the time I had Professor Grant backed against the wall, I was ready to explode. I wanted to be furious that he denied me a fight, but it all fizzled out when I saw the lost look on his face. I recognized that look too well. He, too, was drowning in his own head.

My professor wasn't like other men. He let me take everything I needed so I could feel whole and grounded. In return, I soothed him as best I could, but it wasn't near enough. He tried to play it off when I texted him this morning, but I knew better. Tonight would be different.

"Cassie?" my grandmother called to me from the other end of the table. Her sharp features were exaggerated by the sullen look on her face.

Crap! Did she ask me a question? I had been so zoned out with my own thoughts that I had forgotten I was still here.

"Your grandmother was asking if you have met anyone *special* lately." Aunt Margaret informed me with an apologetic look.

"Nope. Been busy with the start of the new semester," I replied. The lie came out far too easily, but it was one I was used to telling. My love life was something I never shared, much to the old witch's dismay.

"Studies are important, yes, but so is finding the right kind of man," Grandmother said between sips of her mimosa.

The urge to roll my eyes was strong. A quick glance at Aunt Margaret told me she was fighting the same battle. My bitch of a grandmother just couldn't help herself.

The right kind of man was a dig at my father. Grandmother has never been subtle with her dislike of him, which is hilarious to me because she had only met the man a handful of times decades ago.

"When I meet a man worth my time, I will be sure to let you know," I lied with a tight smile.

"Maybe you will meet someone at the Ainsworth Autumn Gala in a few weeks."

Oh, yes, Ainsworth Autumn Gala. Grandmother's opportunity to simultaneously parade the scholarship recipients around for the local media and lord her wealth over the PGU staff.

Ever since I had started college, it also became the night she would shamelessly introduce me to every eligible bachelor in attendance. Her lack of subtlety made the event absolutely embarrassing the last two years.

"The fitting for your dress will be next week. Your Aunt Margaret will make sure you have the details," she continued, making it clear I had no say in the matter.

I gave a small smile and nodded like the good little granddaughter while swallowing the bile that crept into my mouth. I learned early on that it was far easier to play the part than fight the witch, even if it made me sick to my stomach.

After brunch, I took the bus home. Aunt Margaret would have gladly given me a ride, but taking the bus always upset grandmother and I desperately needed to be petty. The woman found so many ways to assert her control over my life that I jumped at any chance to reclaim my power.

The sour look on grandmother's face as she watched me walk toward my stop was food for my soul. If the little things didn't get under her skin, then I never would have survived these last few years. All I wanted to do was give up and run back to my parents, but I promised my mother I would give this an honest shot.

My mom was a sophomore in college when she met my dad. She ended up dropping out so she could get a job and support my father's music career. The scandal of it all enraged my grandmother, and she cut my mother off financially. The move was meant to force my parents apart, but it only made them closer.

My father's band never took off, which Grandmother loved to point out. She saw him as nothing but a failure and refused to hear otherwise. It didn't matter that he became an indie music producer who earned more than enough to provide for his family. Her mind was made up.

Thinking about my parents always made me miss them terribly. Free college was nice and gaining access to a trust fund upon graduation was even better, but the distance from my parents was hard. Most days it wasn't worth the money, but it was important to Mom, so I pushed through it.

Two more years.

The bus ride home gave me a chance to decompress from my toxic Saturday morning. Mellow tunes flowed through my earbuds as the world around me melted away. The worst of the day was over.

Episode 15

First Date

Joshua

Catherine O'Hanna, a name I haven't thought about in a long time. She was my date to the eighth grade formal and the last time I felt this nervous about a date.

Was tonight even a date?

Sweat had poured from my body in buckets as we stood next to each other beside the gymnasium-turned-dance floor. I was terrified she would reach for my hand and then recoil when she felt how slick it was.

Lord knows how I mustered the courage to ask Catherine to the dance in the first place. I kind of blacked out when I approached her with the world coming back into focus as she said yes. Thankfully, there were no gaps in consciousness during the dance, just a lot of painfully awkward moments that I had successfully forgotten until now.

Like my first kiss. At some point, we ended up on the dance floor, slowly swaying back and forth with my hands on her hips and hers on my shoulders. The cheap fog machine and streamers created a weird ambiance that only middle schoolers would find magical. When the song ended, I began to nervously pull away. Catherine had other plans. She pulled me in and planted her lips on mine.

In hindsight, it was a horrible kiss. I had no idea what I was doing, blindly swishing my tongue back and forth while I tried to suck the life out of her. It was not my finest moment, but at the time, it was magical.

Things were different in high school. Dating felt so much easier when girls were practically throwing themselves at me. They were flies, and I was the honey. *Cringy, Joshua.* By the time I pursued Janet, I was an overconfident ladies' man with plenty of experience.

Now? I may as well be that young boy standing in the middle of the gym, too scared to hold his date's hand. I could barely keep a good grip on the spatula while I tried to stir the onions with the way my palms were sweating.

Deep breath, Joshua. Get it together. She won't stick around if you are a human waterfall.

I closed my eyes and took a moment to center myself. The sad truth was my confidence still hadn't recovered from the breakup. I thought everything between Janet and me was fine when she broke it off. Better than fine, actually. We had started discussing a more long-term future together. Then she cut me off without any warning or explanation.

How could I possibly keep history from repeating itself if I didn't know why I failed before? It was a constant fear that whispered to me in the quiet moments. I felt powerless.

Breathe. I counted slowly as my chest rose and fell with every breath. *In, two, three, four. Out, two, three, four.* I had no reason to be nervous. *In, two, three, four. Out, two, three, four.* Cassie was definitely into me if last night was any indication. *In, two, three, four. Out, two, three, four.* I just needed to keep my cool, and everything would be fine.

The initial plan for the evening was to order pizza. It was a simple and safe plan. Everyone loves pizza, right? Things went off the rail when I texted Cassie earlier to find out what pizza toppings she liked.

Goddess: My taste is a bit too obscure. Pepperoni is fine.

Naturally, a response like that got me curious. No one describes their toppings preference as obscure. As it turned out, she wasn't kidding. It took a bit of convincing, but after a little begging, she relented. Pineapple and caramelized onions.

I became a man on a mission, eager to prove that I could provide whatever her heart desired. The need to be praised fueled my search. I would present Cassie her prized pizza, and she would swoon and tell me how wonderful I was.

Unfortunately, the universe decided things would not go smoothly for me. The first pizzeria laughed at me for some reason when I asked if it was possible. After the third pizza joint proved to be useless, I decided to surprise Cassie by making the pizza myself.

The new plan was still simple: buy pre-made crust, sauce, along with the toppings, and put the pizza together myself. The slight detour somehow evolved further and further until the only thing that I wasn't making from scratch was the cheese and dough, and that was only due to time constraints.

As it turned out, pizza sauce was pretty easy to make. It was probably the easiest part of this whole plan so far. The sauce sat on the counter in a dish to cool next to the large Tupperware of fresh cut pineapple chunks. A whole pineapple produced a lot more than what I needed, and I had no idea what I was going to do with the rest of it.

She is going to laugh at you for going overboard.

I shook the negative thoughts from my head and powered on. Cassie wasn't going to laugh at me. Nope. She was going to be impressed. Maybe she would even reward my effort.

I turned my attention to the caramelized onions and gave them another stir. *Almost done, finally.* The onions, while not difficult, were the most time-consuming step. I had spent the better part of an hour preparing them.

— ♥ —

Within seconds of pulling the pizza from the oven, there was a knock at the door. My heart picked up the tempo as waves of excitement crashed over me and washed away the nerves. Cassie was here! My sweet, beautiful Cassie was right outside my apartment.

Eagerly, I rushed to the door to see my sweet goddess. The anticipation had morphed from an overwhelming fear of failure to this indescribable euphoric feeling. Soon Cassie would walk over the threshold and be in my home, eating the food I made for her. My hands shook with giddy energy. I felt like an excited puppy whose master had just come home.

The moment I opened the door, all words left me. She was an absolute vision standing there in a little black dress that showed far more skin than it covered. I stood in silence, my mouth watering, as I admired how the fabric clung to her small curves.

"How do you do it, Professor?" Her sultry voice washed over me, clearing my mind from the lust-filled fog.

"Do what?" I asked.

"Make a T-shirt and jeans look so sexy," she replied with a giggle that almost brought me to my knees.

The corners of my mouth pulled upwards into the goofiest grin, and I didn't even care. Hearing that Cassie thought I was sexy did things to me that I didn't fully understand. I shamelessly adjusted my stance in the doorway, hoping to give her a better view. Yes, I was preening like a lovesick fool in hopes that she would give me more of the praise I so desperately craved.

Another light giggle fell from those beautiful pink lips, drawing my focus right to them. My mind fogged over again as thoughts of those lips on my cock the night before bombarded me. I needed to feel her lips on my body again.

"Are you going to invite me inside, *Professor*?" Cassie asked as the tips of her fingers trailed down my chest.

I gasped with a sharp intake of breath, involuntarily flexing as her touch traced just above the waistband of my jeans. *Focus, Joshua.* My pants felt tight as my growing erection obeyed the call of its mistress. *She asked a question. Focus.*

"Huh? Oh! Right! Um, please come in," I offered awkwardly as I stepped to the side. *Way to go, making her stand in the hallway.*

Her familiar scent of cherries and vanilla danced past me as Cassie stepped inside. I had to fight back the groan that threatened to come out as I drew a long breath. She had no idea how crazy her fragrance made me. My cock was so fucking hard for her that it was a struggle to keep my hands to myself.

I turned to close the door, using the opportunity to adjust the bulge in my pants. My control hung by the thinnest thread, ready to snap at any moment. I needed to get my excitement under control. Spending the evening with a constant erection would be both uncomfortable and embarrassing if Cassie noticed.

With a deep breath, I forced myself to calm down. *Don't fuck this up after all your hard work! Just be normal.*

"Welcome to my home. You have great timing. The pizza just came out of the oven," I said as I turned back to Cassie.

She tilted her head as her brow furrowed with a strange expression in response. *Fuck.* Had I already screwed up somehow? That couldn't be possible as all I did was let her inside.

"The pizza was in the oven? I thought we were getting delivery? Did it arrive cold or something?" she asked. The way her nose scrunched up in slight disgust was so adorable I couldn't stop my chuckle.

"No. No. It didn't arrive cold. I decided to skip delivery when no one had what you liked. I know you said pepperoni would be fine, but I found a pretty easy pizza sauce recipe online and—"

"You made the pizza yourself?!" Cassie's eyes widened in surprise.

"Most of it. I mean, I bought the crust ready to go because I wasn't sure I could manage that, but I made everything else from scratch. I can't wait for you to taste the caramelized onions. With that said, I have a lot of pineapple left over," I rambled on, both proud and embarrassed.

As great as it felt to have Cassie here in my home, the faint nervousness was still there, just below the surface. I had become used to her taking control of our interactions, relieving me of the pressure of possibly screwing up. She wasn't jumping in to take control, and it left me second-guessing every decision I made earlier in the day.

My eyes dropped to the ground as I anxiously scratched the back of my head. There was no need to share about the overabundance of pineapple, but I couldn't stop myself once the words started to flow out of me. More and more of my excitement was transforming back into nervous energy, and I wasn't sure how to move forward without making a bigger fool of myself. I was drowning in a sea of anxiety and insecurity.

"Joshua," Cassie called to me softly. Her fingers gingerly guided my chin until our eyes met. The soft look in her eyes as she gazed up at me melted away all thoughts. My body relaxed as I let myself surrender to her gentle command for my attention. Each breath was lighter without the pressures from before weighing down on me.

I had never been into blue eyes until I met Cassie. Janet's were light brown. It was one of the things that drew me in initially. As I stared down into Cassie's, I couldn't fathom why I would ever like any other color.

"You are beautiful tonight. I don't think I said that out loud yet," I said in reverence.

The faint blush that colored her cheeks was as captivating as the rest of her. Overcome with a feeling I didn't fully understand, I dropped to my knees and wrapped my arms around Cassie. Eyes closed, I nuzzled into her and took a moment to enjoy the peace she brought me. Each breath filled me with cherries and vanilla. She consumed me in every way.

"Thank you." Her melodic voice washed over me as she ran her fingers through my hair. "And thank you for going through the trouble of making the pizza I like."

While I couldn't see Cassie's smile with my face buried against her body, I could hear it when she spoke. Her happiness was a reward within itself.

"Nothing that makes you happy is trouble, Cassie," I replied, still holding on to her.

Our current position reminded me that we still needed to have a conversation about our relationship dynamics and expectations. *Relationship.* Dropping to my knees unprompted should have sparked some sort of remark, but Cassie never questioned it. She let me anchor myself without any judgment.

"If you think the pizza has cooled, I am famished," Cassie said, pulling me from the spell I was under.

"Of course," I said as I rose to my feet.

While dusting off my knees, embarrassment trickled through me. *You just dropped to your knees and clung to her like a teddy bear.* But Cassie didn't seem to mind, and she even stroked my hair.

"Where do you keep going when you do that?" Cassie asked.

"What do you mean?" I said, trying to play dumb.

"You go quiet and then you look so sad."

It was too soon to open up about the last few months. You never unload your ex-girlfriend baggage on the first date, and this was technically our first date. Or as close to one as we could have under the circumstances.

I took a step forward and grabbed her hand. There was a connection between us I had never experienced with anyone else. Touching her gave me strength when I felt weak.

"Sometimes I get lost in myself. Please don't ask me why. Not yet, anyway." *Maybe not ever.*

Cassie studied me for a moment before she spoke. "Fine. But only if you make a real effort to stop. You look like you are hurting when you do that. I don't want you hurting."

I stood in awe for a moment as I digested her words. She didn't belittle what I was experiencing by treating it like a switch I could flip on and off. She didn't demand I spill my secrets. No, she asked that I make an effort... *Because she doesn't want you hurting. She cares that you are hurting.*

She cares. That filled parts of me that I didn't think could be reached again. I thought I knew all the scars Janet left behind by now.

"I will work on it," I promised.

Hand in hand, I led Cassie to the kitchen. There was a need to keep some form of physical contact with her. The connection kept me focused on her instead of wandering aimlessly in my own thoughts.

She gave my hand a quick squeeze as we entered the kitchen. Though it seemed to be more for her benefit than mine. For the first time, I noticed a slight bounce while she stood like she was trying not to fidget.

Despite the occasional immaturity expected of someone her age, Cassie possessed an impressive confidence. At least, that was what I assumed. It never occurred to me that Cassie would be nervous, too.

"Oh, wow! It looks and smells amazing!" Cassie gushed as she dropped my hand and rushed over to the pizza. The look of pure hunger on her face as she ogled the pizza filled me with pride. She was practically drooling over it.

"Thanks. I just hope it tastes good, too," I laughed. *God, that was lame. Just shoot me now.*

"Like something that smells this heavenly could taste bad," she responded with that beautiful smile of hers.

I grabbed a couple plates and began to serve up.

The dining room table was covered with assignments and other papers in an effort to make it appear unusable. The plan was a bit overcomplicated, but I felt like I needed an excuse to eat at the little bar area that overlooked my kitchen. It was the perfect opportunity to cuddle closer to her.

Sitting closely on the bar stools, her leg casually brushed against mine. The thrill of the friction coursed through me. It was exactly as I planned.

I watched eagerly as Cassie took her first bite. She moaned in delight as she savored it. The sounds she made were quite filthy as she savored another bite. I wasn't sure if I should've been flattered or turned on. *Both.*

My mind began to conjure images of Cassie on her knees, making those same sounds while her lips were wrapped around my cock. Maybe I could even convince her to swallow next time. My dick loved that idea, stiffening at the thought.

"Dude, Joshua. This has to be the best pizza I've ever had," Cassie mumbled with a hand raised to hide her mouth full of pizza.

I wasn't sure what was more amusing, the way Cassie spoke excitedly with her mouth full or the fact that she just called me dude. I couldn't stop the laughter from spilling out of me, almost choking on my beer in the process. Cassie shot me a warning look that had no bite to it when paired with her beautiful smile. This was what I had been missing for the past few months.

"So, Josh-u-a..." Cassie paused and took a swig of her beer. "What made you decide to become a college professor?"

"I just kind of fell into it," I answered honestly.

"How?" She tilted her head and watched me with curiosity.

"I went to college with the intention of becoming a professional writer. Writing was my passion. It still is. At some point, though, I lost confidence in myself. I no longer wanted to share my work with others. The thought of someone reading what I wrote terrified me. Unfortunately, I was already well into college by the time I decided to bail. Education seemed like the easiest transition. No idea if it really was. Not a very noble answer, I'm afraid." I had never said any of that out loud before. It felt strange yet freeing. It was like a weight had been lifted, and I could breathe a little easier. How long had that been weighing me down, and I didn't even know?

"You think you gave up on yourself?" she asked. Her head was still tilted slightly, but her chin was now propped up by her hand. The way her eyes squinted as she watched me, almost as if she was studying me, caught me off guard.

"In a way, yes. Honestly, I don't think about it too much anymore. And after meeting you, I can't say I'm disappointed with how things turned out," I replied with a chuckle.

As corny as it sounded, it was the truth. Meeting Cassie changed me, or at the very least, our meeting sparked the healing process I had been fighting. I had spent far too long worrying about failure in some way, shape, or form. All that fear was holding me back. I was able to see that now because of Cassie's presence.

"You may change your mind once you get to know me better," she teased. There was a glimmer of sadness in her eyes that caught me off guard.

"I seriously doubt that, Cassie. Sure, you are a bit demanding, but I seem to enjoy it," I teased, hoping to bring back her smile.

Cassie was my sun, the bright warmth in my universe. I needed to learn how to be her rock and bring her the same clarity among the chaos that she provided me.

"Yeah, I had no idea you would actually be into that when we met. I was expecting you to leave me in the bathroom," she said with a laugh.

"I had no idea, either," I confessed.

"Really? I find that hard to believe. You are a natural at dropping to your knees." She licked her lips, her eyes trailing over my body.

"Only for you."

Suddenly, Cassie was off her stool and standing between my legs. Her hands gripped my thighs possessively in a move that made my breath stop. My goddess had my complete attention as she leaned in and pressed her body into mine. She was so fucking close, but I needed her closer. I needed her naked flesh on mine. My body ached for it.

I reached up, desperate to feel her soft skin, but stopped as I re-membered I had not been given permission to touch her. With Cassie so close to me, I was not going to risk breaking any unspoken rules. Instead, I kept my eyes locked on hers as I waited for my goddess to make her move. Her hands began to rub my thighs.. The bulge in my pants was too prominent not to notice, but Cassie didn't acknowledge it other than stopping just before contact each time her hands stroked upward.

My naughty little goddess was testing how far she could tease me before I snapped. That was fine. I could be a good boy and behave even if it was slowly driving me insane. My legs spread a little wider, giving her the space she needed to lean in further.

"I just realized you never gave me a tour of your place. That was a bit rude, don't you think?" Her lips quirked upwards into a small smile, mere inches from mine, as she spoke in a breathy voice. Her hooded gaze dropped to my mouth as she pulled back slightly and awaited a response.

The question was code, but I didn't mind. Cassie wanted to play and for once, I knew the rules. It was finally happening. The moment I had been waiting for since that night in Florida. All I had to do was play along, and I would finally experience heaven. Easy enough, right?

"Forgive me, goddess. That was rude of me, wasn't it? Would you like a tour now?" I answered softly. I held my breath in anticipation even though I knew the answer. It was the waiting that made the game fun.

Cassie took a few steps back, causing the black fabric of her skimpy dress to sway with each step. Her mischievous look as she bit her bottom lip was almost enough to make me lose control. Somehow, I stayed in my seat and watched patiently as those delicious lips began to part.

"*Yes.*"

Episode 16
The Main Event

Joshua

Cassie's legs wrapped around me as I pressed her body against the wooden door. She was like an animal in heat, the way she clung to me while her body wriggled and writhed against mine. My sweet goddess wanted me. No, she needed me. That thought wormed its way into my brain and ignited something primal in me.

Don't worry, Cassie. I'm here to make that needy ache feel better.

So far, the tour tour had entailed the two of us locked in a passionate kiss while our hands roamed each other's bodies, and I blindly stumbled towards the bedroom. The journey had progressed only slightly smoother once I lifted her into my arms. Her tight grip on my hair mixed with mine on her ass made it difficult to focus, thus why we were on the wrong side of the door at the moment.

A wild moan escaped Cassie, her head tilting back as she arched her breasts into me. Her nipples, hardened from arousal, poked through the layers of fabric. My mouth watered, eager to strip her down and suck on those perfect breasts.

Our steamy hallway make-out session was driving me closer to the edge. My cock strained against my jeans, desperate to bury itself in Cassie's warm, wet cunt. I had been waiting to feel her wrapped around my dick for so long, and now I was only a few steps away from making it a reality. It was almost too much.

Soon.

I needed to find my calm before I completely lost myself to the lust-filled craze I was drowning in. The only thing holding me back from ripping off her clothes and fucking her on the floor was the same thing that sparked these feral urges in me. As much as I needed to find my release inside Cassie, I needed it to be good for her, too. A cheap floor fucking was below my sweet goddess.

A twinge of pain throbbed at my scalp as Cassie tightened her grip on my hair and pulled me into another passionate kiss. It was forceful and hungry, her tongue demanding entrance. I was all too happy to surrender and let my goddess take all that she wanted from me.

Cassie rolled her hips in a steady rhythm as her tongue danced wickedly inside my mouth. It was her body's plea for me to worship at her temple until her needs were sated. *Maybe a floor fuck wouldn't be so bad.* A sharp sting ran through me as Cassie dug her nails into my shoulders. It drew me from my euphoric haze enough to nix the floor idea yet again.

I needed to focus. And make it to a bed. We had somehow made it further down the hall than I realized. The wall I had Cassie pressed against was actually the door to the bedroom. *Thank you, universe.* All I had to do was pause our kiss long enough to get her inside the bedroom.

I pulled back to speak, only to let out a long moan when Cassie began to suck on my neck. The pleasure pumped through my body as if it had been injected directly into my veins.

"This is the bedroom door," I said, somehow, between heavy breaths. It was a lame attempt at a joke made worse by my distracted delivery.

"It's a lovely door. Care to show me what is on the other side?" Cassie quipped breathlessly.

That was the goal, but it required setting Cassie down, and I couldn't. My entire body revolted at the very thought of relinquishing my hold on her. She was mine, which meant she belonged in my arms, but the longer I refused to budge, the longer I delayed the main event. It was a conundrum that was next to impossible to solve with Cassie grinding against me.

"Hold on tight," I whispered as one hand tightened its grip.

Cassie interlocked her fingers behind my neck while her legs tightened their hold around my waist. Confident she wouldn't fall, I reached out a hand blindly in search of the handle.

After fumbling for a minute, I found the cool metal of the doorknob. Mid turn of the handle, Cassie's lips pressed into mine. I leaned into the kiss, pushing the door open in the process. With the loss of support, I stumbled forward, almost dropping the precious treasure in my arms.

"Careful, Professor," Cassie whispered. A shiver of need ran down my body in response.

"Of course, my sweet—"

Buzzz. Buzzz. Buzzz.

I froze as something repeatedly vibrated in my pants. *You have to be fucking kidding me right now.* This was the worst moment for someone to call me. *Should have put the phone on silent. Too late now.*

"Your pants are vibrating," Cassie giggled.

"That they are," I huffed as I gently placed her on the bed.

Whoever was calling had the absolute worst timing. I didn't even bother to check who it was before I turned the damn thing off and tossed it aside. The chances of the call being an emergency were almost zero. It was likely my mom doing one of her random check-ins. I would probably get an earful later for not answering, but a chat with Mom was not what I was in the mood for right now.

"That was a little disappointing. I thought you had a surprise for me," Cassie pouted. The playful little minx was jutting out her lower lip in an exaggerated fashion that was more adorable than it should be.

"Sorry. No special toys tonight, but if it is something you're interested in?" I said as I cocked an eyebrow.

Cassie's cheeks blushed a bright pink that betrayed the innocence she tried to hide around me. "You are different, you know that? Most guys get jealous if I even joke about a vibrator."

"Then you have been hanging around the wrong men. I am not threatened by silicone. Anything that aids me in making you come over and over is more than welcome in the bedroom. And if I'm being honest, the idea of watching that tight pussy of yours stretch around an obscenely thick toy while I fuck you with it sounds hot."

Cassie's eyes glassed over with lust as her lips parted. It was magical watching her work through the words until the pink had spread well beyond her cheeks.

Relief washed over me, seeing her react positively to the suggestion. I had often made similar suggestions to Janet, and while she always said she would be down to try things, she never came across as sincere about it. It made me too uncomfortable to follow through.

The vision of a woman before me was completely different, though. Offering to fuck her with a dildo had Cassie almost drooling. She watched me with hungry eyes, not apprehension. If anything, she looked excited.

"I want you naked," Cassie commanded with a sultry voice. Fuck, why did her giving me orders make me so fucking hard?

"If that is what you wish, my goddess," I replied, trying my damnedest not to sound too eager.

Finally. Finally. Finally. The words repeated over and over inside my head. This was it. First my clothes, then hers, and then I would finally get to experience all the carnal pleasures her body has to offer. *Have to get naked first.* My heart was beating a mile a minute as I reached down for the hem of my tee. My fingers were barely grasped around the fabric when Cassie beckoned for my attention by clearing her throat.

I turned to give Cassie my undivided attention, curious as to what made her interrupt such an important task. There was a devilish look in her eyes that told me she was scheming something. *Hopefully something fun.*

"Take your time. Make it a show."

I froze in place like a deer in the middle of a dark highway with the lights of a semi barreling towards it. Make it a show? How was I supposed to make it a show? Did Cassie expect me to dance around like the Chippendales men? *Wait, are they even a thing anymore or is it all* Magic Mike *now?* Either way, it wasn't something I felt I could pull off. Cassie didn't need to see how little rhythm I had. This was one request that I would have to decline.

"Um... I don't think—"

"Good. It would be better if you didn't," Cassie said as she adjusted her position on the bed. I was about to argue, but the smile she flashed me pulled the fight right out of me.

Cheeky girl. As much as I hated to admit it, her sass did the trick. With my nerves gone, I dove headfirst into my "routine."

There were no grandiose moves. I didn't swivel my hips or thrust in the air. That wasn't something I could do. I only removed my clothing at a more leisurely pace than I originally intended and hoped that was enough.

The tension melted from my muscles as I watched Cassie watch me. The look of pure desire that burned in her eyes as I slowly removed my shirt was intoxicating.

"You look so delicious. I can't wait to taste you," I said as I tossed my shirt on the floor.

"You want to lick me, Professor?"

I loved how Cassie teased me, playing as if she had more self-control. But I saw the little tells, like the way she squeezed her thighs when I spoke, or the way she held her breath as my fingers hovered over the button on my jeans.

"I'm going to do so much more than that, my goddess. I am going to take my time and worship every inch of your body the way it deserves." Her eyes followed as my zipper slowly trailed down. "You will be a soaking mess of pleasure before my cock sinks deep into your sweet cunt."

"Big talk, Professor." Her taunt would have carried more weight if she wasn't watching my pants drop to my ankles like a lioness about to devour its prey.

There was something magical about the way Cassie watched me. The hunger in her eyes wasn't an uncommon experience for me. Plenty of women ogled me, but it was different with Cassie. There was no shame, frustration, or disgust. It was the complete opposite. I was filled with a confidence that hummed through my body that allowed me to stand tall.

"We both know I am skilled at making you come, Cassie. Now, do you want to see what you watching does to me?" I asked as I stroked my cock through the fabric of my boxer briefs.

"Stop teasing and drop them." The command spilled from her like honey, thick and sweet.

When the goddess that holds your leash gives you an order, you have no choice but to obey. I removed the last article of clothing as fluidly as I could. Cassie clapped her hands and cheered as my erection sprang free. My cheeks burned, no doubt bright red from embarrassment. I had never received applause for undressing before.

That's not true. That one time in college, rush week... Nope. Not what I should think about right now.

I stalked towards Cassie before she could make another request. As much as I loved to pretend otherwise, patience was never something I was good at. I had plans, and they were to sink my rock hard length into her warm, wet pussy.

Step one was complete. Now was the time for step two. I crawled onto the bed and hovered over my sweet goddess, caging her body with mine. My cock wept as it rubbed against the fabric of her little black dress, creating a small wet spot.

"You have far too much clothing on," I said with a dark smile.

Cassie's fingers trailed the contours of my muscles as they grazed over my chest. The way she couldn't stop herself from touching me was driving me insane.

"Then do something about it."

That was all the permission I needed. I lifted Cassie's dress over her head, exposing lingerie so obscene that I almost came right then. The bra, if you could call it that, consisted of a few ribbons of fabric crisscrossed around her chest, barely covering her breasts. The tiny thong wasn't much different.

I had spent most of the day worrying whether or not we would make it to this point. Cassie had clearly planned for this outcome. To wear something so impractical meant there was never a question in her mind. She knew she would end the night in my bed.

"You are trying to kill me," I groaned as my finger lightly grazed along one of the ribbons. It was tight, much like the threads of my self-control.

"Don't like it?" She teased me in a voice that was far too innocent. Cassie was anything but innocent.

"Just the opposite. You are such a fucking temptress, hiding this surprise during dinner. *Fuck.*" My brain had officially left the building. It took every ounce of focus I had to maintain my control.

"I thought I was a goddess?" Cassie asked with a raised brow.

"You are. Now let me worship your body, my naughty little goddess."

She let out a giggle as I trailed kisses down her neck. The cheery sound vibrated through my body until every cell was alive with want. Only Cassie could make a giggle sound erotic. Or maybe I was too far gone to register any feelings other than carnal need.

My lips made their way down her soft body until I reached her perfect breasts. I hooked my finger under one of the taut ribbons and pulled it back to expose the hard nipple it barely hid. Cassie moaned and her body arched closer as I clasped my mouth around the nub and sucked.

The filthy sounds that came from Cassie as she wiggled below me were delicious. I swirled my tongue as I sucked, determined to tease more blissed-out moans from her. She fisted the sheets as I moved my attention to the other breast, eager to give it equal attention.

While I distracted Cassie with my mouth, my hand traveled down to her pussy. When I reached her thong, it was soaked with her arousal. If Cassie was already this worked up, it wouldn't take much to push her over the edge.

The fabric covered so little that I didn't need to remove it to gain access to her folds. Cassie whimpered as I slipped two fingers inside her with little resistance. I had not been allowed this level of access to her body since our first night.

It was heaven to be permitted back inside her and made better by the improved location. My bed was the altar on which I worshiped my goddess. I had no plans to stop until the sheets were soaked with her release.

My fingers continued to pump inside Cassie while my mouth alternated its attention between her breasts. Every moan of ecstasy, every squeeze of her cunt, was like a drug and I was high as a fucking kite. Her pleasure pumped through my veins, driving me to find my next fix. Nothing existed except Cassie.

"Oh, Professor!" Her cries of pleasure filled the small bedroom when my thumb circled her clit. Every moan and mewl that poured from her was a siren's song that called out to my very soul.

New goal, make Cassie moan so loud the neighbors hear her through the walls.

Sharp nails dug into my shoulders as Cassie began to push me downwards. I didn't need her words to understand what she wanted, and I was more than eager to obey. Slowly, my lips trailed her body, caressing her skin with soft kisses as I traveled downward.

I channeled all of my focus on Cassie and her pleasure. It had been hard at first to push aside the need that coursed through me like fire, but now it was nothing more than a dull ache. This was my purpose. Nothing else mattered as long as Cassie was squirming on my hand.

The first flick of my tongue had Cassie's hips rising off the bed. A feral growl worked its way through me as I continued to feast on her delicious cunt. How I had starved for this moment. Now, nothing would stop me from devouring her pussy until my hunger was sated.

Cassie laced her fingers through my hair, forming a tight grip. It was all the reminder I needed that I was not the one who decided when I had my fill.

Cassie's muscles started to lock up. Her thighs hugged my head while her grip on my hair became almost painful. I ignored it, focused purely on driving her over the edge.

With a curl of my fingers at just the right moment, Cassie exploded. A screech of unbridled euphoria drowned out all other sounds as she broke from the pleasure. The way her body crashed through her climax was almost enough to make me blow my load.

The way her pussy continued to spasm around my fingers as I kept my pace steady was magical. This woman was made for me to pleasure. I continued to finger fuck her through the little aftershocks until Cassie whimpered and twisted in an overload of sensations.

"Stop!" she pleaded as she tried to back away.

Cassie whimpered and shivered as I slowly removed my hand from her pussy. My fingers were dripping with her sweet release. Our eyes locked as I pulled them to my mouth and licked each one. Not a drop of her would be wasted.

"That..." Cassie paused to take a breath. "That may have been better than last time."

She plopped her head back on the pillow as her body went limp. The post-orgasm haze was taking effect. *I did that.*

"I'm glad you enjoyed it." I was more than glad. I was ecstatic. Any praise from her filled me with pride. After the show I just witnessed, I was practically overflowing with it.

"I most certainly did. That performance definitely deserves a reward. You have condoms this time, right? Or do you only keep them in your office?"

"Funny, Miss Jones," I teased back.

The box of condoms I hastily purchased when I got back from Florida was too big to keep in my nightstand. I had placed one in my wallet and dumped a few in the drawer of the nightstand for easier access. Now that I was staring inside the drawer, I realized that I may have gone a bit overboard. Inside was a plethora of square foil wrappers in all sorts of colors. They filled halfway up the space, if not more. No woman would think this many condoms was normal. *And there are more in the closet.*

I grabbed one at random and slammed the drawer. The last thing I needed was for Cassie to know that I hoarded condoms. There was no way to explain them without sounding desperate.

The bed shook behind me, drawing my attention back to Cassie. She had shimmied out of the miniscule lingerie and sat naked, waiting. I flashed the little square package and gave her a smile.

"Nice! Now, hand it over and lie on your back," she instructed as she reached out with "gimme" hands. I had to hold back a chuckle at her adorable eagerness.

Cassie snatched the foil from me, inspecting it as I adjusted myself per her request.

"Monster condoms... Oh! These are those funky new ones that glow in the dark." She squealed in excitement.

Wait. What?

"I'm sorry, monster what?" I asked. *There is no way. No. No.*

"Oh, Josh-u-a. Didn't you pay attention to what you were buying?" She teased. The mischievous devil's eyes sparkled with delight at my discomfort. *Glad someone finds it funny.*

I was far too embarrassed to admit that I grabbed the box because it was the biggest one, but no believable lie came to mind. That left me naked on my bed with a very panicked look on my face. *Definitely not sexy, Joshua.*

Cassie rolled her eyes as she smirked. At least someone was enjoying themselves, because I certainly wasn't. Every bit of confidence I had gained tonight drained from my body.

"Don't give me that look. It isn't a big deal. I think they are kind of fun."

"Because they glow in the dark?" I asked in disbelief.

"That, and they are all different colors and themes. Looks like this one is called Swamp Monster," she said as she read off the packaging.

Just when I thought things couldn't possibly get any more humiliating, Cassie ripped open the foil and pulled out the day glow green latex ring. A shudder worked through my body as I tried to stay calm. There was no way Cassie could think something like that was sexy. My cock was going to look like a glowing cucumber. *Or Swamp Monster.*

"It isn't the mood killer you seem to think it is Joshua," Cassie insisted as if she could read my mind.

"I guess. I just don't see the appeal in a neon green *Swamp Monster*," I replied in a huff of defeat.

"Then let me show you. But first, we need to get you back in the game," she said as she began stroking my cock back to fullness.

Great. I went limp, too. Way to keep it going strong, Joshua.

My eyes closed as I focused on Cassie's soft touch. That green monstrosity was not going to ruin my night. If Cassie didn't care, then I shouldn't either. It was that simple. I just needed to stop thinking about the damn thing.

"Your face is all scrunched and unhappy, Joshua," Cassie's sultry voice cooed. "Get out of your head or I might have to *punish* you."

My body relaxed immediately, scared into submission by her gently delivered threat. This time, I successfully blocked out all distractions. There was only Cassie.

Her hand lightly stroked my cock. The soft touch teased me back to fullness with the promise of what was to come.

"That's better. *Good boy*." And just like that, my cock was awake. More than awake. Those two beautiful, magical words had me as stiff as a flagpole. But that wasn't enough for my goddess, she wanted to play some more.

Soft lips pressed against the head of my cock, sending a shock of pleasure through my system. My eyes popped open, eager to watch my goddess at work. She looked deliciously filthy as she licked me like a lollipop. Her flattened tongue worked me shaft to tip, over and over. Her eyes locked onto mine as she licked, daring me to continue watching.

"Fuck. Cassie, keep that up and I won't last long," I rasped as I thrusted on reflex.

Cassie responded by deep throating my cock. The feel of her mouth engulfing me was maddening. This really was going to be over soon.

My body felt a frustrating sense of loss as she pulled off my cock with a lewd pop. "No coming without permission, Professor. Understand?"

"Yes, my goddess," I lied. I knew it was a lie, too, but what else was I supposed to say? This entire night was one close call after another. There would be very little control once her tight pussy was wrapped around my cock, condom or not.

Pleased with my obedience, Cassie rolled the condom over my erection. I focused on the feel of her hands, the sight of her naked body, anything I could that would distract me from the bright green phallus that was now my cock. If nothing else, she seemed amused by it.

The way Cassie straddled me was a beautiful sight. She looked like a queen about to take her throne. I watched with bated breath as she lowered herself onto my cock at an excruciatingly slow pace. My body begged for me to thrust into her and take control, but I knew better. This was not the time to test boundaries. Instead, I tried my best to relax and enjoy the moment.

My hands gravitated to Cassie's hips, steadying her as she sheathed my cock in her pussy. I held her in place once I was buried to the hilt, wanting to enjoy the feel of her around me. Her body fit mine like a snug little glove. It was an indescribable bliss that I wanted to experience forever.

For a moment we just existed, connected to each other. Then, Cassie began to move her hips, and the universe came alive around me. My fingers dug into her as pleasure crashed over me like a wave. She wasn't bouncing on me like a porn star, no. Cassie was grinding her hips, using me to chase her own pleasure.

Never had I experienced a woman reduce me to an object that she could take from like that before, and it was divine. I was merely a vessel for her enjoyment, a toy.

The friction from her movements was different from anything I had experienced before. My body felt like it was balancing on the edge, but unable to take the final leap. The smell of sex and sweat filled the air as she became more frantic in her movements, but it was never enough.

My restraint snapped, and I thrust into her in earnest. Our moans echoed off the walls as we fucked like a pair of rabbits in heat, our rhythm perfectly in sync.

My balls tightened as the pressure built. It wouldn't be long now. *Not without permission*. Fuck.

"I...I can't much longer." The words stumbled out of me a jumbled mess. Unable to form a coherent sentence, I switched between "Please" and "Cassie" over and over.

"Yes!" Cassie screamed out as her nails clawed down my chest. Before the word fully registered, her cunt began to pulse around my cock.

My vision went white as my own climax tore through my body with a roar of satisfaction. Every muscle in my body strained as I emptied myself into Cassie until I was tapped dry.

The lust-fueled haze that had been driving me dissipated with my orgasm. I was left a sweaty mess, void of all thought and energy.

With the little bit of strength I had left, I pulled Cassie against my chest and held her tightly. We could clean ourselves later. She cuddled into my hold, a sign she needed this too. And so we lay there together. And for the first time in a long time, my mind was at peace.

Episode 17

Two Best Friends

Eddie

"No, you didn't! I don't believe you. Nuh-uh." Carla shook her head in disbelief as she threw a few pieces of caramel popcorn at me. They bounced right off me and landed on the tacky maroon carpet she loved so much.

"I swear it. Cross my heart," I said with a smile as my fingers drew an X over my heart.

"Two girls at once? How did you manage that?" Her eyes widened with surprise. She leaned in with bated breath. No doubt she was expecting some elaborate and steamy tale that was porn worthy.

My calm mask of indifference began to crack little by little. Carla looked so damn cute with that expression of naïve curiosity plastered all over her face. She leaned even closer as she waited for me to calm down enough to continue. I couldn't hold back any longer. Laughter poured out of me like a burst pipe.

Carla crossed her arms with a huff. She didn't find the situation nearly as amusing as I did. Or maybe she was just impatient.

"Honestly? The story is going to disappoint you, sweet cakes," I said, wiping a tear from my eye.

"I still want to hear it. Or it didn't really happen," Carla insisted. *Because that's really how things work.*

My hands raised in faux defeat. The only way this conversation was going to move ahead was if I indulged her curiosity.

"We were playing spin the bottle at a party in high school. Bonnie spun the bottle, and it stopped right between me and Maddie. Well, Bonnie was going to spin again, but I stopped her and said that she had to kiss both of us at the same time," I explained with a shrug.

"You. Did. Not." Carla gasped with amusement.

"I did."

"And they agreed to?" she asked skeptically.

"Not at first, but my buddy Kevin backed my suggestion and then they caved," I replied with a big, shit-eating grin.

"Oh my god, Eddie. I can't believe you. How was it?" This wasn't the reaction I had expected for such a lame story like my triple kiss. I hoped Carla wasn't getting any ideas for happy hour on Monday.

"Awful. I don't recommend a triple kiss. It's just messy chaos," I told her honestly. No reason to lie about it.

Now it was Carla's turn to burst into a fit of laughter. I just sat back and watched as her tight, brown curls bounced with her like they were laughing, too. It was a sight I could only enjoy when we hung out away from work. In the office, she always kept her beautiful curls locked down in some tight updo to appear more professional. I personally hated it, and not just because I thought her wild hair was beautiful. I also hated that she felt like she had to mold pieces of herself to fit in with the office culture.

"I've missed this," Carla said as her laughter subsided.

"Me too," I agreed.

She wiped away a stray tear as she took a calming breath. Her cheeks were still flushed from all the laughter and it made me wonder if that is what she looked like after—

Nope. Stop that. We do not think about Carla like that. She is a friend, not some random fuck. I quickly pushed those thoughts right out of my head.

"Why is it never just the two of us anymore?" Carla asked as her laughter subsided. Straight to the point tonight. And here I was, hoping to get through the night without any heavy conversations.

The couch suddenly felt lumpy and uncomfortable, or maybe it was her question that had me squirming in my seat. The truth was there was no single answer and none of them made for a decent excuse. But Carla expected an answer and I wasn't in the habit of lying to her.

I grabbed a handful of caramel corn and shoved it into my mouth. It was an obvious stall tactic, but I needed a moment to think.

We may have been friends for a while, but I still remember bumping into Carla on her first day at BranTech Security. The bright-eyed data analyst somehow ended up in the corporate sales department on her first day. That was some feat, considering our departments were separated by a few floors.

She seemed so nervous that I offered to give her an impromptu tour while I escorted her back to her wing. Turns out she had gotten off on the wrong floor after lunch. Lucky for Carla, I knew every department pretty well. Finding where she belonged was a piece of cake. By the time we reached her desk, Carla and I had bonded.

Have you ever met someone and just clicked with them? I don't mean in a romantic way. Like in the movie *Step Brothers*, how a switch just flipped, and they were best friends. That was Carla and me after that first day. She joined me and the rest of my sales crew most days for lunch. I conveniently found excuses to stop by her desk most mornings.

It wasn't long before we started hanging at the posh bar next to work for happy hour. Then, weekend movie nights with just the two of us, but it was always just as friends. No, more than friends. We were best friends.

It wasn't that surprising we had become so close. My other dear friend wasn't the ride or die I had thought he would be. That wasn't an entirely fair assessment of Josh and my friendship. I'm sure if something truly horrible happened, he would be there for me, no questions asked. The thing was, best friends were so much more than that. When he reconnected with Janet, everything shifted. If I wanted to spend time with him, then I had to spend time with her.

Carla, on the other hand, never made me hang out with any of her boyfriends. Sure, I met a few of them, but it was never forced if I wanted quality time. My girl even went a step further and joined me when I hung with Josh and Janet so I wouldn't be a third wheel. And the way she handled the harpy so I could actually spend time with Josh was just amazing.

Joshua! He is the perfect excuse. At least it wouldn't be a lie.

"I'm sorry. I've just been worried about old Joshy-boy. He took the breakup really hard. Annoyingly hard, really," I said. Was it shitty to throw my friend under the bus like that? Nope. After being subjected to Janet all those years and then his mopey ass for an entire summer, it seemed more than fair.

Carla gave me one of her looks as she picked up her hard cider and began to chug. The way her head tilted back, exposing her bare neck, was magical. I wanted to graze my teeth along her skin and see if she would whimper for me.

And where the fuck did that thought come from? Jesus man, get your mind out of the gutter! For the second time, I was shifting uncomfortably on the couch, but this time was to hide my growing erection.

"I call bullshit," Carla said as she placed the bottle back on the coffee table.

"What?" I asked, truly lost. *Fuck. What were we talking about?*

"If you have been worried about Joshua, then what was last night?" There was no bite to her question, but I still flinched at the accusation.

She was right. Last night was a big lapse in judgment on my part. I knew better than to drag Joshua to a college hot spot, but I wasn't thinking about him at all when I planned it. Bowling was supposed to be just Carla and me. She had dropped hints about wanting to go for a while now. The only reason I made Joshua tag along was because he had been acting a little off lately, and not the post-breakup sulking kind of off.

"You're right. Dragging him along to our bowling night was a mistake. If I had known you were going to flirt with him, I would have let him stay home and wallow, sweet cakes," I said before I could stop myself.

Fuck. Why? Why did I say that? I wasn't even thinking about how she threw herself at him. There was no reason to bring it up out of the blue like that. *Fuck.*

"Excuse me?" *Now you've done it, Eddie.* Carla was not amused by my accusation at all. The scowl on her face said I was mere moments away from trouble.

The smart thing to do in a situation like that would be to back down and apologize. It was the only thing to do if I wanted to keep our friendship intact. Unfortunately, my mouth wasn't getting the memo.

"You were obviously flirting with him when we got there. Not a great idea, trust me. It has been months since he got dumped and he still hasn't recovered. You don't want to jump into bed with a guy like that."

Carla let out an adorable huff of frustration. She needed to quit doing that because it was making it hard to focus on our conversation.

"We will tackle your jealousy in a moment. I was referring to how miserable he was with all the girls catcalling him. It really made him uncomfortable, Eddie."

Record scratch! Did she just say jealous? I was not jealous. Sorta. I mean, I was jealous in a broader sense. Joshua always had women throwing themselves at him. Always. I get why the students made him uncomfortable, but they weren't the only ones. It was a bit infuriating how he would complain about the attention when we would go out, like throngs of women ready to just open their legs for him with no real effort was some sort of curse.

Last night was not about jealousy, though. It was pure concern for Carla. Knowing how Joshua was, I didn't need her getting her feelings hurt when he rejected her. Then I would have to punch my best friend in the face for making my other best friend cry, and that just sounded like too much drama.

"I wasn't jealous," I tried to argue. "You know I support your right to sleep with whoever you want, sweet cakes, but he would not be a fun time right now." Or ever. "I know Joshua probably seems like the sexy kind of sad right now that makes you want to mend his broken heart with crazy sex, but he isn't. He is just the 'no fun' kind of sad. Trust me, I just spent an entire summer watching him sulk."

"Who mends a broken heart with crazy sex?" Carla asked. Not the response I expected, but a welcome topic change.

"Um... who doesn't? That's what rebound sex is," I replied.

"Rebound sex doesn't have to be crazy," Carla insisted as she rolled her eyes. *Speak for yourself, sweet cakes.*

"Why would you waste rebound sex with something vanilla? That is just a waste," I scoffed.

Carla stared at me for a moment, her pouty lips slightly parted, no doubt ready to put me in my place. I braced myself for whatever lame argument she was going to drive her point home with, but it never came. She turned away and sank deeper into her side of the couch.

That wasn't a good sign. The conversation had veered off course to the point that I couldn't remember where it started, and Carla looked upset. *Way to fuck up the evening, Eddie.* There had to be a way to fix this.

I scooched myself next to her and tapped her knee with mine. "Ignore me. Of course, not all rebounds are crazy kinky."

"But yours are." It wasn't a question, which struck me as odd.

The only time I shared those kinds of details was when something outlandish happened. *Like horse girl*. It wasn't nearly common enough for her to make those kinds of assumptions. Plus, I wasn't known to keep long-term pussy around.

"Not exactly? Rebound sex implies there was a breakup that preceded it. I'm more of a one-night stand kind of guy. You know that," I said as I placed a hand on her knee.

"But your one-night stands are wild and crazy."

And just like that, my hand recoiled. Where the fuck was this coming from? The conversation had taken another detour, one that made me really uncomfortable.

"It was a joke, Carla. You know I'm rarely serious about half of the shit that comes out of my mouth."

"You kissed two girls," she countered.

"When I was a teenager. C'mon, what does that have—"

"Have you had a threesome?" She blurted the question, effectively shutting me the fuck up.

The thermostat jumped twenty degrees easily, making the room uncomfortably hot. Or maybe it was the heat from Carla's intense stare that had me sweating. This was supposed to be a casual night of drinking, not "grill Eddie on his sexual history" night.

"Where is this coming from all of the sudden?" I asked in an attempt to take the focus off of me.

There was a dangerous look in Carla's eyes as she turned her body toward mine. The smile that crept over her lips filled me with lust and fear. My body couldn't seem to decide if we were terrified or aroused.

"Oh. My. God! You have, haven't you?!" The excitement in her voice was overflowing. Why was she so delighted?

Maybe she wants a threesome? No. Nuh-uh. Not going to happen. First of all, I do not see Carla as a sex object. I definitely hadn't been fighting the urge to rub one out to the bikini picture she sent me last month. That would be wrong. And even if I was into Carla like that, which I wasn't, there is no way I would share her. But it didn't matter, because we were just friends. Better than friends, even.

"What? Are you ashamed you had a threesome? That seems like the kind of thing guys brag about." Who was this girl and what did she do with my sweet Carla?

"At the time I was," I confessed for some reason. My mouth desperately needed a filter.

"But not now? What changed?" she asked curiously.

"It isn't even that I'm not proud now," I tried to explain, "more like I just don't ever think about it. I was in college. You know how crazy it is in college."

Everyone had crazy college stories. Getting wild in college was like a rite of passage. Even Josh got his freak on. A lot actually, now that I think about it.

"No, I don't. I didn't have the crazy college experience everyone else seemed to have. I went to community college, then transferred to the state university to finish up my degree, all while living at home with my parents. My summers were spent picking up whatever classes were available so I could graduate early and move out. Not a lot of time for the *college experience*. Hell, I didn't have sex until I was twenty-nine!" she said as she threw her hands in the air.

There were no words. None. I mean, what on earth was I supposed to say after that? Carla and I had been friends for years. She was so ingrained in my current life that I had forgotten that a time before us even existed. Probably because we never talked about the *before*. Why would we? There was never a reason until now.

"Twenty-nine, huh?" I said in a poor attempt to fill the awkward silence. *Shut up, Eddie. Why would you say that?*

Carla's eyes widened as her expression morphed into something scared and sad. It was like nothing I had ever seen before. Her hands rose to cover her face in a weak attempt to shield herself. Did she see me as a threat?

"Fuck! Why did I tell you that? That is so embarrassing." Her voice strained over the words.

A tightness in my chest began to form as irritation boiled inside me. The frown she hid poorly was like a knife repeatedly stabbing my heart. The longer she was unhappy, the more I bled.

"Carla, sweet cakes, look at me. Please?" I leaned closer and gently grabbed her hands.

Glossy tears welled up in the corner of her eyes like a dam about to burst. I had only seen Carla cry once. The man responsible was quick to apologize after a brief conversation with my fist. I didn't know what to do this time. There was no one to punch.

You know exactly how to fix this, Eddie. Fuck. I did. I hated that I didn't hate the solution.

Carefully, I pulled Carla into my lap and wrapped my arms around her. The scent of her shampoo invaded my senses as she nuzzled her face into my chest, conjuring images of frolicking through a meadow.

The minutes passed by in silence. Neither of us moved aside from the small, calming circles I rubbed on her back.

This was dangerous, very dangerous. *But it feels right, doesn't it?* No. *Liar*. Fuck.

"Did I miss my chance?" Carla asked, breaking the silence. Her voice shook as if she was still fighting back tears.

"Miss your chance for what?" I asked softly.

"The wild and crazy sex phase," she mumbled into my shirt.

Well, Eddie, you walked right into that one.

"Why would you even think that, Carla? You are never too old to try new things." I tried to reassure her.

"It's just... I don't even know where to begin. What should I do? Make a list of all the things I want to try?" A huff of frustration left her as her shoulders sagged.

A list? I quickly squashed the laughter that bubbled inside me. Only Carla would think she needed to make a sex list.

"That is one way to go about it, I guess," I said, unsure how else to respond.

"Will you help me?"

"What? Make the list?" That sounded like a recipe for disaster. It would no doubt involve me having to relive cringy sexcapades from my past.

"No...well, yes. That could be helpful. But I was hoping maybe you'd help me past that... with the items on the list..."

No.

No. No. No. Definitely not. That was a line we could not cross. Not now, not ever.

"Of course." *God fucking dammit*! Why? Why would I say that?

My head was spinning as my thoughts raced. The knot in my chest grew tighter and tighter until I could barely breathe. There had to be a way to back out. I just needed to explain that I misspoke. I merely meant I would help make the list and nothing more.

"Really? You don't think it's a dumb idea? Or that things would get weird between us?" Carla asked as she stared up at me, all doe-eyed and hopeful. My resistance melted away like snow in the summer. Only a monster would deny this woman anything.

"It will be fine. Besides, you'll want someone you are comfortable with for something like this." This being sex. *Wild, crazy, kinky sex.*

The brightest smile danced across her lips as she clapped her hands in excitement. I had been a fool. Nothing that made her this happy could be bad.

Carla began to gush excitedly about our new agreement, but the specific words were lost on me. I was far too captivated by that smile. Those plush lips were a work of art when she smiled. How had I never noticed before?

Swept up with the sudden urge to feel those lips on mine, I leaned in and silenced Carla with a kiss. Her body stiffened for a fraction of a second before she relaxed into my body.

Slow and sensual, our tongues danced together as heat sizzled through me. I was drowning in a meadow of wildflowers, as if that was even possible. With Carla, it apparently was. This kiss, this moment, it was the answer to a question I didn't even realize I had.

We pulled apart slowly, neither daring to speak and risk bursting the magic of the moment. Instead, Carla silently readjusted herself in my hold so she could face the TV.

I locked my arms around her when she reached for the remote, an unknown fear of her leaving my arms taking hold. The hairs stood on the back of my neck as I mentally worked through a solution that kept her where she belonged.

Carla didn't question or tease when I finally leaned in and grabbed the remote myself. She seemed more than content to stay cuddled in my embrace. *Good.* The elusive unease that trickled through dissipated with Carla's unspoken compliance. I once again felt at peace.

We stayed in our strange little bubble while a movie droned on in the background. There was no more kissing, no more talking. We just sat there and existed and all was right with the world.

At the end of the night, we said our goodbyes as if nothing had happened. It wasn't until I sat in my car with the key in the ignition that the gravity of the night's events began to weigh on me. A thick sludge of dread filled my lungs, making it impossible to breathe.

I agreed to fuck Carla. No, I did more than that. My chest ached as I forced myself to breathe. I agreed to fuck Carla repeatedly in all sorts of unknown ways.

The stale air was not nearly enough to calm me. My vision blurred as panic took root and anchored itself in my very soul.

Joshua! Joshua would know what to do. At the very least, he could talk me off the ledge I was on. I fumbled through my pocket and pulled out my phone. With shaky fingers, I dialed my friend and waited.

Voicemail.

"Seriously? We both know you aren't doing anything. I need to talk to you. Now." My thumb smashed the red button on the screen with far more force than necessary.

Fuck!

Episode 18
Uninvited Guests

Joshua

As the night progressed, I may have gotten a little overzealous in making Cassie come as much as possible, not that she complained. My greedy little goddess had been rather encouraging, even demanding at times. Just thinking about the way she commanded me was more than enough to get my dick stirring again.

At one point, Cassie was ass in the air, squeezing my cock with her tight cunt as I thrust into her. Despite the traditional power dynamics of our position, she had complete control. My thick length was throbbing as I begged her for permission to come. She kept me fighting my climax until I was almost crying in pain, but the endorphins that flooded my body post orgasm when she praised me for obeying put me in a euphoric state. I was so eager to chase that high that I dove between her legs with no resistance when commanded moments later.

Being with Cassie was different. I had always been the one in charge of deciding the if's and when's of my partner's pleasure. It was a heady feeling having that kind of control over someone, but it was nothing compared to the intoxicating bliss of relinquishing control. Following orders meant that my mind was free to focus on drowning in pleasure. Hers, mine, it didn't matter.

After another long, sweaty session, I led Cassie into the bathroom to clean up a little. It was getting late, and we both needed rest after exerting so much energy.

A small pang of guilt poked at me as I noticed her steps falter occasionally. Her energy was waning faster than mine. I had assumed between her youth and the enthusiasm she had displayed that everything was fine. Watching her sluggishly make her way down the hall proved I was wrong.

"The vampire was a bit more red than I had expected," Cassie confessed. The soft slur in her voice only confirmed that she needed to rest.

"I looked like a glowing tube of lipstick. We are not using that one again," I huffed with annoyance. Cassie only laughed in response. *At least someone finds it amusing.*

With Cassie barely able to stand, a shower was out of the question. My beautiful goddess was far too precious to risk slipping. Instead, I laid a plush towel on the counter before setting her on top.

Those delicate fingers of hers traced the contours of my arms as she gave me a dark grin. Goosebumps rose along my skin with each spark her touch created. I knew Cassie was trying to tease my body into reacting, but now was not the time to play.

"*Professor.*"

A shock of arousal ran down my spine as the word fell from her lips. I was seconds away from dropping to my knees so I could feast between her soft thighs.

Focus!

My body trembled as I tried to contain my lustful urges. The hungry look in Cassie's eyes was not helping, either. It was one thing to deny myself, but it was another to disobey.

She hadn't given an order. Yet. She can't sit up on her own.

The internal struggle had my self-control hanging by a thread.

"Please, Cassie." The words came out slightly pained as my body tensed. Was I asking to stop or keep going?

The tension held for only a second before Cassie acquiesced, her fatigue winning out over her carnal hunger. My body protested the loss of her touch as she released my arms and leaned back against the mirror. It was a necessary evil if I wanted to accomplish anything, but I didn't have to like it.

My muscles tensed with frustration as I began fussing about the bathroom, grabbing a washcloth and soap. I had a task to perform. The sooner it was over, the sooner I could cuddle her in my warm bed.

"You're good at this. It doesn't make sense," Cassie mused quietly, exhaustion heavy in her voice.

"Hm? What doesn't make sense?" I asked as I ran my fingers under the water to test the temp.

"All of it. How has some beautiful woman not snatched you up?" she said with a yawn.

The innocence of her comment drew a smile from me. Did she truly not see?

"A beautiful woman did snatch me up," I replied as I soaked a washcloth under the warm water.

"What happened?" she asked with a slight frown that deepened as I chuckled. Why did her jealousy warm me? I shouldn't be so pleased.

"I was talking about *you*, Cassie."

A beautiful blush crept over my goddess's bare body, reminding me that we were both still very naked.

Focus, Joshua! She needs rest.

Focus was easier said than done. Memories of earlier flooded my mind as I trailed the warm cloth over her bare skin. The way she moaned when I fucked her with three fingers. The way she whimpered as I licked her well beyond her climax. Focus was impossible. By the time I spread her legs, my cock was a steel rod.

A slight shiver ran through Cassie, effectively breaking the spell. Lust was immediately replaced with shame. My sweet goddess needed me to take care of her, not use her for my own selfish needs.

Once clean, I took great care to towel Cassie dry and carry her back to my room, where I dressed her in one of my shirts and boxer briefs. There was a small thrill in seeing her wrapped in my clothes and tucked in my bed. It was a subtle act in claiming her as mine.

My arms held her firmly against my chest as she slowly drifted off to sleep. Utter contentment swelled inside me despite the dark shadow of reality that crept towards my happy moment.

Enjoy while you can. She won't be in your bed every night. But she was here now, that was what mattered. Tomorrow could wait until tomorrow.

She lay peacefully in my bed, a smile on her lips as her chest rose and fell with steady breaths. Cassie was deep in sleep now. Deep enough that she didn't stir as I slowly removed myself from the bed.

As much as I wanted to stay with her, the kitchen was still a mess and I was still sticky with sweat and sex.

Carefully, I checked the blanket Cassie was wrapped in. She looked far too peaceful to disturb, but I needed to make sure she would stay warm until my return. Her golden mane spread across the pillow, much like Sleeping Beauty. *Mine.*

My body protested as I left the room, angered at the growing distance between us. More necessary evils.

A shiver ran through me as I stepped on to the icy linoleum floor of the kitchen. Normally, I wore socks in my apartment during the autumn and winter months due to the chill that always hung in the air. I hadn't thought to put any on tonight, though. Most of the evening, I had been preoccupied with tending to Cassie with my own needs falling to the wayside.

Are you sure she is warm enough in your room?

If Cassie was going to be spending more time here, then I needed to make sure my apartment was more prepared. Tomorrow I could go shopping for a few more blankets to be safe. Maybe I could even surprise her with those fuzzy socks. There were a few sweatshirts I never wore anymore hidden somewhere in my closet. Girls loved to steal their boyfriends' sweatshirts.

Boyfriend. That word brought a smile to my lips. Would Cassie refer to me as her boyfriend?

I was floating on a cloud of joy. Everything felt lighter as I moved through the kitchen. Wrapping pizza in tinfoil wasn't rocket science. I was able to perform the task with ease while I plotted my future with Cassie. How often could I convince her to stay over? Week nights might not be the most appropriate because of classes, but surely I could talk her into spending the weekends here. Maybe not every weekend, but still—

"Seriously? This is what you do when I leave you on your own?" A deep voice called out from the entry of the kitchen.

I let out an embarrassingly tiny shriek as the box of tinfoil dropped from my hands.

"Jesus Christ, Eddie! What the fuck? That key is for emergencies!" I whisper-yelled, anger slowly boiling inside me.

My fist clenched and unclenched beside me as I tried to rein in my emotions. This was my time with Cassie. Eddie's presence felt unwelcome, like he was invading my territory.

"And I am experiencing an emergency. You would know that if you picked up your damn phone. Do you know how many messages I left?" he asked as he tapped his foot impatiently.

Well, now I know who called.

"It's on silent, Eddie. I've been busy," I informed my friend as I bent over to retrieve the fallen tinfoil.

"I can see that. Really had a craving for pizza while butt-ass naked, huh? Maybe you could throw some clothes on. This isn't college, buddy," he said mockingly.

I froze, bent over with the box of tinfoil in my grasp. Eddie was right, I was as naked as a jaybird. *In your own home.*

My skin felt hot as I slowly stood up, though I was unsure if it was from anger or embarrassment. *Why not both?* With a frustrated sigh, I grabbed the kitchen towel and covered myself as best as I could.

"Really? Sure you don't want to go grab some clothes?" Eddie asked, unamused.

His flippant response had me seething. This was my home. I was free to wear as little as I wanted to, dammit!

With Cassie asleep in the bedroom, I needed to keep my temper in check. The last thing I needed was for her to wake up scared or come out here while we had uninvited company. I needed to get Eddie out of here quickly and quietly.

"Why go grab clothes if you're going to be leaving? I told you I'm busy. Take the hint, Eddie," I snapped a little louder than intended.

Silence. Eddie didn't argue or poke fun at how utterly ridiculous I looked with a kitchen towel covering my junk. He just stood there expressionless, silent. This wasn't right.

He said it was an emergency... Fuck.

With a deep breath, I walked back my frustration. *An emergency.* Eddie didn't know I had a girl over. It wasn't his fault that I had been keeping him in the dark about Cassie.

"I'm sorry. What happened?" I asked, my eyes cast down in shame.

"I kissed her."

Kissed... her? Her who?

I locked eyes with Eddie, brow furrowed in confusion. That was not the response I had expected.

Unsure who or how a kiss constituted an emergency, I tried to clarify. "Okay? Her being?"

"Carla, man. I kissed Carla! Why the fuck did I do that?" Eddie said as his arms flailed wildly.

Breathe. Carla. He kissed Carla. *Breathe.* The asshole barged into my apartment and snuck up on me because he kissed Carla. *That asshole is your friend.*

"Are you serious right now?" I asked curtly.

My hand throbbed as my grip tightened around the small towel that covered my cock. Annoyance over his immaturity was slowly morphing into rage. This *emergency* was not worth keeping me from the goddess in my bed.

"Right? But it gets worse, Josh. I agreed to have sex with her, too! Like, fuck! What is wrong with me?" Eddie began to rant.

Oh, the list I could have made at that moment.

"First, not so loud. Second, I don't see what the problem is. If anything, I'm surprised it took you this long to ask her out."

"I didn't ask her out. Why would I ask her out?" he asked like an idiot.

Oh my fucking—

A sharp pain started to throb behind my eyes as I tried to decipher what in the fuck this conversation even was right now. This was not how my wonderful night was supposed to go. I should have been in bed with Cassie, cuddling as we slept. Instead, I was stuck listening to Eddie complain he kissed his crush.

"Let's walk this back a little. You and Carla kissed," I said slowly, desperate to appease him so he would leave.

Eddie stared at me in response, like I was the idiot in the room. Me and not the guy freaking out over a kiss like it was the four horsemen of the apocalypse.

"Yes. We had been talking about her sex list and how she wanted my help."

My brain stopped listening, stuck on the sheer ridiculousness of that statement. I was clearly trapped in a nightmare, unable to wake.

"Eddie, I am going to stop you right there. It is late and I am far too sober to help you unpack any of this right now—"

"You have to be kidding me! Really, Joshua? Really?! I am having a crisis, and you don't even fucking care, do you? I would never shove you off like this." The words echoed through the kitchen.

Deep breaths, Joshua. He is your friend. My fingers pinched the bridge of my nose in a feeble attempt to thwart the oncoming headache. I needed to defuse the situation and get him out before he woke Cassie.

"I'm not trying to shove you off. It's late and this doesn't sound as dire as you think. If you sleep on it, I'm sure you'll see that." I tried to reason.

"You really don't get it, do you?" Eddie asked coldly.

I only shrugged in response, unsure what on earth I was supposed to say. This whole tantrum of his had spun out of control.

"I've already lost you. Once this all blows up in my face, I'll lose her, too." The faint panic in his voice was like a knife to my heart. How could Eddie possibly think that? *Because you're kicking him out.*

"Eddie, what are you going on about? You haven't lost me."

"Haven't I? You haven't been the same since Janet. She's not even around anymore! She dumped your ass in May. MAY! It has been four months and look at you!" The anger dripped like venom off every word he spewed at me.

My vision went red the moment he said *her* name. *How fucking dare he!* My body shook with rage I could barely control. How dare he invoke her name. How dare he belittle what I went through when he was having a panic attack over a goddamn kiss.

That was the last straw. The dam broke open, and all fury spilled out.

"I know you can't understand because your *relationships* never last more than a weekend, but Janet and I were together for YEARS! Forgive me for not immediately being all sunshine and fucking rainbows! Now GET THE FUCK OUT!"

All the color drained from my body when a soft voice joined the conversation. "Who is Janet?"

Episode 19

The Plot Thickens

Cassie

"Who is Janet?" I repeated a little louder when neither man answered.

Honestly, *Janet* was the least of my concerns. The way Professor Grant eyed me like a starving dog with a steak dangled in front of him most days, I doubt she would be any real competition.

The real problem was the scene I walked in on. Some guy I vaguely recognized was in the kitchen with my very naked professor. He looked positively terrified standing there with a small dish towel clutched tightly in his trembling hand. It was the only thing that gave him any coverage.

I couldn't tell from Joshua's expression if it was my interruption or the other man that was unwelcome. It left an uneasy feeling in my stomach. Could I even compete with another man? *Time to buy a strap-on.* I wouldn't even know what to do. *Sure you would. Just imagine the professor bent over...*

"Holy shit! You're Florida girl!" the unknown man exclaimed, shattering the silence and my newest fantasy.

If looks could kill, the man would have been dead. All the excitement from his discovery drained as he shriveled under my glare.

That's right. Know your place.

"Florida girl's name is Cassie," I snapped.

Did I recognize him from Florida? No. I had no idea Joshua had been with anyone else that night. So where? *The bowling alley last night.* Yes! He was flirting with the lady they were with. *So probably not a threat.*

"I. Um. Okay, sorry," he mumbled uncomfortably. I shouldn't have derived so much pleasure from watching the man squirm, but I couldn't help it.

"Say it," I commanded, a little drunk on the rush of power that was flowing through me.

The man's head snapped up, eyes locked on to mine as he seemed to contemplate his next move. A small grin appeared as he relaxed a little.

"Sorry, Cassie. I didn't realize Joshy-boy had company," he said, the grin growing bigger by the second.

Joshy-boy? Who the fuck was this guy?

I turned my attention to the professor for answers. The poor man looked like he was seconds away from a full-blown panic attack in his kitchen. That wasn't good.

You need to anchor him. No shit, self. But how? *On his knees seems to work.* Yeah, no. I was not going to order my English professor to drop to his knees while naked when we had an audience. *Clothes.* That was a good place to start.

"Give me a second," I said with an annoyed sigh before I headed back to the bedroom.

None of my questions had been answered so far, and it was getting under my skin. I couldn't hide my aggravation as I stomped into the bedroom, my blood pressure rising with every step.

Who was the man in the kitchen? Why was Joshua naked? And who the fuck was Janet? *Sounded like an ex.* That thought made me pause. Did he still have feelings for her? The idea left a bitter taste in my mouth.

You just have to make him forget her. Sure. Easy. But first, pants.

I picked up the discarded pair of jeans, dropping them back on the floor almost immediately. They didn't seem nearly comfortable enough. Right now, Joshua needed something comfortable.

Bet *Janet* never took care of him like this. *Assuming you can.* I definitely could. I just needed to find comfy pants.

The closet?

I thought men were supposed to be messy, but nothing about this man hinted at the stereotype. His closet was very organized. *Very organized.* I almost felt bad for messing it up as I rummaged around.

"Bingo." Gray sweatpants, man's sluttiest piece of clothing. I grabbed a pair and headed back to the kitchen. *Is that for him or you?* Both.

As I got closer, I could hear the two men whisper back and forth.

"I didn't know you would have company. It's not like you told me about her."

"You say that like I was keeping her a secret on purpose."

"Were you?"

Men.

"Pants," I called out as I tossed the pair to Joshua.

"Thanks," he said, putting them on as soon as he caught them.

Clothed, his body relaxed as the tension eased from his muscles. My gaze lingered as I admired how good the professor looked in gray sweatpants and rumpled sex hair. He appeared as the same calm, confident man I swooned over during class, only shirtless and dripping sex.

My eyes trailed up his toned body until they locked with his. The smug grin on his face made me blush as I realized I'd been caught.

Joshua sauntered over with a confident swagger that perfectly fit the fantasy of him. The sexy professor charming his way into his students' beds, except I was the only one. His arms wrapped around me, pulling me into a lovingly possessive embrace, letting me know he felt the same. I wanted this man back on his knees, worshiping between my thighs.

Got to get rid of the other guy first. Ugh. That's right.

"So... Now that you have pants on, want to introduce me to your friend?" I teased with a half-hearted smile.

Joshua's expression dropped as his brow pinched in frustration. With a slight shake of his head, he sighed in resignation before giving the introductions.

"Eddie, Cassie. Cassie, Eddie."

Eddie huffed as he rolled his eyes. He then turned his attention to me, flashing the smile expected from a used car salesman. It wasn't creepy or sleazy, but it wasn't genuine either.

"It is truly a pleasure to meet you, Cassie. I should apologize for intruding. Josh never mentioned he kept seeing you after that night," Eddie said, tossing Joshua a judgmental look.

There were definitely layers to the tension between these two. It was going to take the finesse of a bomb technician to keep them both from exploding.

"We only just reconnected on Monday, so he wasn't keeping secrets," I said, hoping the explanation would diffuse the situation a little.

"Though we do need to keep this between us, Eddie. I can't exactly let it get out that I'm involved with one of my students," Joshua added.

With eyes wide, Eddie opened his mouth, but no sound came out. It was comical watching the once loud intruder reduced to a silent, gaping fish.

Joshua didn't share my amusement, apparently. His hold on me tightened.

"Dude, I am sorry I didn't listen to you at the bar—"

"I'm not," Joshua growled, taking his friend by surprise.

"Be a good boy and calm down," I teased softly, without thinking.

I didn't need to see his face to know if he heard me. The cock growing stiff against my back told me everything. The professor *really* liked being called a good boy. A lot from the feel of things.

"Sorry," he continued calmly, "I'm just not upset. If anything, I'm grateful you pushed me into it."

"Grateful enough that you can spare some time to help me with my crisis?"

"Eddie, it's not a crisis. I promise you everything will be—"

"Why not a late breakfast tomorrow?" I cut in. "Pick up a couple to-go platters from Tiffany's Pancake House, and we can work through whatever is bothering you."

Eddie just stared at me like he wanted to object. This was going to drag on forever if I didn't seal the deal.

"Do you want someone who will take you seriously? For the low cost of a pancake breakfast and ride home after, your crisis will be treated with the utmost urgency. Tomorrow."

"He's upset because he kissed a girl," Joshua said dryly.

"And that is a huge problem that needs our full attention. Tomorrow. And after we solve it, Eddie can drop me home so I don't have to Uber the day after in that little black dress. In the meantime, Eddie can go home, and we can continue with our evening. Everyone wins," I said, entirely too cheerful. *You're overselling it, Cassie.*

Eddie rubbed his chin in contemplation for a moment before he shook his head and laughed.

"I think I like you, Cassie. You've got yourself a deal," he said as he reached out a hand.

I eagerly accept, sealing our deal with a handshake. *Perfect.*

Once the details for the next day were settled, Joshua quickly ushered his friend out the door. The air immediately felt lighter once it was back to just the two of us.

"Eddie, huh?" I said as I lifted myself on to the kitchen counter.

"Sorry about that. He has a key that is supposed to be for emergencies only," Joshua explained.

His eyes cast downward to the floor as he ran a hand through his hair. There was something magical about the vulnerability he displayed in the moments we were alone.

"And the emergency was he kissed a girl?" I asked incredulously.

"Yeah, Carla. She's super sweet. Great at handling him. I think he is just afraid because he hasn't really liked someone in a long time." He looked wistful as he spoke, and it made me feel bad for Eddie.

As sad as it was, I couldn't say I was surprised. Our brief encounter had me convinced the man had the emotional maturity of a teenager. Not many women his age would have time for that kind of headache.

A calm silence stretched between us. Joshua stood between my legs, and his fingers traced little circles up and down my thighs. He seemed more than content to enjoy the moment, but I still had questions I wanted answered.

With a delicate touch, I lifted his chin until our eyes met. Never had a man looked at me with such warmth and affection. It made me feel...

Scared. Yes, scared. I had only really known this man for a week. Despite Professor Joshua Grant's infamy around campus, I had been blissfully unaware he even existed before this semester. And yet here he was standing in front of me, looking at me like I was the sun and the moon. It terrified me.

So why did I despise the thought of him looking at another woman the same way?

Because you are selfish. You want him all to yourself. The attention excites you as much as it scares you. You love the power he lets you wield over him.

No, not power. Control. My time with Joshua was the only time someone else wasn't telling me what to do. It wasn't selfish to want control over your own life.

"You're the one lost in thought for a change," Joshua said with a smile.

He leaned in and placed a tender kiss on my nose. The moment was so sweet and perfect that I almost stopped myself from ruining it. Almost. But I needed answers. I needed reassurance. I needed to know the rug wouldn't suddenly be pulled out from beneath me when I least expected it.

"You never told me who Janet was." The words felt like acid on my tongue.

Joshua's reaction was almost exactly as I expected. He froze in front of me as sadness clouded his eyes. Janet was obviously a sore subject, but that only made my need for answers greater. His face twisted with a multitude of emotions, pain, hurt, fear, until something darker took hold.

"Because she doesn't matter," he said coldly. All the warmth and love was gone as he stared right past me. It was like I wasn't in the room anymore.

"I heard you say that you had been with her for years, so I'm assuming she's an ex. At least, I hope she's an ex." The thought slipped out unfiltered.

"Yes, she's my ex. I told you before that there was only you," Joshua said. His fingers dug lightly into the soft flesh of my thighs, silently begging me to stop.

Careful, Cassie. Proceed with caution. Fuck caution.

"Why not just say that and be done with it? Or do I need to worry about her?"

You would have thought I slapped him in the face by the look of betrayal he gave me. It wasn't my fault, though. He was the one who kept acting all weird when she got brought up, like he still had feelings for her.

He worships you. And I bet he worshiped her, too. *Your insecurities are showing.*

"Why won't you believe there is only you? I have willingly played along with your little games. What more can I do?" Joshua pleaded softly, almost broken.

Little games. Is that what he thought all this was? Little games?

Episode 20
Foot, Meet Mouth

Joshua

"Little games?!" I flinched as Cassie's frustration echoed throughout the kitchen. *Way to fucking go. Can't blame this one on Eddie.*

Watching her eyes glisten as she fought back tears made me nauseous. The conversation had spun out of control, and I had no one to blame but myself. Cassie was feeling insecure. She needed reassurance, not me lashing out. I needed to fix this before Cassie decided to walk out the door and never come back. The very thought sent an unpleasant chill through my body. I couldn't survive another rejection. Without the light from my sweet goddess, I would descend back into the darkness.

You should have just explained the situation with Janet. No! That would have made things worse. If Cassie knew how utterly wrecked I had been before her... No woman wants a man who is pathetic. *No woman wants a man who insults them.*

Unsure what to say, I tripped over my words, trying desperately to undo my earlier mistake. "I don't mean it like that. I like the games or do you call them scenes? It's not really role-playing—"

"Wait. Wait. Wait. Hold up. Scenes? Games? What are you talking about?" Cassie asked, cutting off my ramblings. It was a bit of a relief because I was floundering helplessly.

Taking a deep breath, I tried to reevaluate the situation. Cassie was looking at me with her brows pinched together with concern. She appeared more confused than angry. Good. That was a start in the right direction, sort of. The night was still salvageable as long as I proceeded with caution. If we continued down this path, then maybe she would forget about Janet for now.

"The dynamics of our relationship. You giving orders, me obeying. I've never really been, um, submissive," I clarified.

Her eyes widened in shock as her mouth silently made an O shape. My heart sank. Of all the reactions I had expected, shock was not one of them. My heart began to beat like a jackhammer as the familiar feeling of self-doubt wormed its way back inside me. Just how badly had I misinterpreted things?

Calm down, Joshua. You're overthinking things. Doubtful. I just insinuated what we had going on was more than basic power play, and she responded with surprise. This is mortifying. *At least she isn't yelling.* But is this any better? *Just walk it back. No big deal.* That's right. This is no big deal. The whole point of having this conversation was to work out the kinks.

My chest was tight, making the huge inhale almost painful. I could do this. Just apologize for misunderstanding and move on.

"I'm sorry. I just thought—"

"No, it's okay. I guess it kind of is? I... I'm just embarrassed because I wasn't even thinking of it like that," Cassie said with a thoughtful expression.

"What were you thinking?" I asked, genuinely curious. The more I knew, the easier it would be to give her what she wanted.

Cassie didn't look at me as she spoke, keeping her eyes cast down at her lap where her fingers fidgeted. "Honestly? This is going to sound dumb, but I have been pushed around by so many people for so long. I just wanted to feel like I had some control in my life."

My heart broke watching the girl who usually radiated confidence shrink into herself. How foolish had I been? I'm a forty-year-old man who barely knows what he is doing day-to-day. How could I expect a girl in her twenties to have shit figured out when I didn't? I reached out, clasping my hands around her in an attempt to offer comfort.

"Does it help? You feeling like you have control, I mean." My voice was calm and steady, a sharp contrast to the unease that flowed through me. *Keep it together, Joshua. Be her anchor like she has been for you.*

"Actually, yeah. It does. Last night at the bowling alley, for example. Jonathan kept pushing and pushing. Nothing abrasive, just enough to make it feel like I couldn't assert my boundaries without being a bitch, ya know? I felt so frustrated and helpless. Then we had our moment out back. It gave me a sense of control like I wasn't drowning anymore." Cassie looked up from our hands and gave me a weak smile. My sweet, vulnerable goddess.

I gazed down at Cassie with a warm smile as I squeezed her hands in reassurance. It was a mask that hid the anger bubbling inside me at the mention of *his* name. The man I had thought of as competition was, in reality, a nuisance. If I hadn't let my jealousy cloud my vision before, then I might have seen it sooner. *Better late than never.* True enough, and now that I knew, I could do something about it. Jonathan was going to learn his place.

"What about you?" Cassie's soft voice cut through my jealous fog, bringing me back from the darkness.

"Hm?" What had we been talking about? *Dammit.*

"Are you okay with how things are going? Because '*little games*' makes it sound like you're not?" she asked, raising an eyebrow.

I winced at the barb. My poor choice of words was evidently going to be thrown back in my face repeatedly tonight. *Whose fault is that?* Things were finally starting to calm down, though. I needed to choose my words carefully if I wanted forgiveness.

"I shouldn't have said it like that. I really am sorry, Cassie. If I didn't enjoy things, then I wouldn't have continued this. Or at the very least, I would have fought you for control. In fact, I find handing over the reins to be rather freeing. It is a lot easier to please a beautiful woman if she gives me detailed instructions," I replied in earnest.

Were there more layers to my sudden love of submission? Definitely, but I was trying to veer the conversation away from my last relationship and how it completely destroyed me. This conversation was about us and no one else.

For a moment, Cassie sat silently and considered my answer. The tension slowly melted away as her shoulders relaxed and she sat a little straighter. The Cassie I knew was coming back to me.

"I'd accuse you of lying, but you do seem to enjoy being on your knees," she teased with a giggle. That beautiful sound was more than enough to elicit a smile from me in return.

"That I do, my goddess," I replied with more heat than intended. It couldn't be helped. Just the suggestion of dropping to my knees made my mouth water for her.

Freeballing in a pair of sweatpants had its disadvantages, like being unable to pretend I wasn't sporting an erection when trying to have a serious conversation. I should have been embarrassed by the obvious tent I was pitching, instead, I was strangely proud.

Cassie bit her lip as her eyes trailed down my body and stopped at my prominent bulge. She squeezed her thighs together as her mind became just as distracted as mine.

The pull of her body was too much for me to resist. I tugged her to the edge of the counter and spread her legs as I leaned in to place what was meant to be a chaste kiss on her lips. Cassie had other plans. The moment my lips made contact, she took over. Her tongue invaded my mouth, devouring me until I was overwhelmed.

My hands gripped her hips, fingers digging into her flesh as I slowly thrust my throbbing cock against her. The few layers of clothing did nothing to dull my pleasure. It was a tease, much like her.

A frustrated growl left me as Cassie broke our kiss with a mischievous grin. She knew all too well how to string me along, dragging out each temptation.

"Now that we've established how much we enjoy our roles, why don't we head back to *bed*?" Her sultry voice danced over me as her hand began to palm my cock over my sweatpants.

My hips rolled as my body reacted on its own, seeking more pleasure. Heading to the bed sounded like a great idea, but the bedroom was much too far at the moment. My mouth watered for a taste of her now, not a minute from now. Just as I began to sink to my knees and bury my face between her thighs, I realized she was distracting me from an important conversation I wanted to have. The conversation *we needed* to have.

"Fuck. Dammit," I cursed under my breath with frustration.

"What's wrong, Professor?" Cassie asked in her sexy little bedroom voice.

I took a step back, giving myself the space I needed to clear my head. *Fuck me for being the adult right now.*

"Before we go any further, we should set some rules," I said as calmly as I could. My body was fighting the distance between us. Every cell in my body screamed for her touch, but I knew that if I gave in, this talk would never happen.

"Like?" Cassie asked with a tilt of her head.

My eyes dropped to her mouth, where she bit her kiss-swollen bottom lip. This was going to be a challenge if she didn't stop taunting me.

"Like no more erotica assignments, for one." The words stumbled out distractedly, with my attention still on her mouth. Fuck, I wanted to kiss her again.

"Fair enough. Anything else, Professor Grant?" she asked with a cheeky grin before sticking out her tongue. *Tease.*

"During class, we keep it professional." The look she shot me said that boundary would get some push back. *Great.* "I'm serious. Neither of us can afford to get in trouble. Keep it professional during class."

"But outside of class, you'll do as I say?" she asked.

Yes!

"Within reason. I'll be the first to admit that I seem to have a problem telling you no. It would be nice if you didn't take advantage of it," I said in earnest.

"No promises," she teased, her voice almost a whisper.

Her playful pushing had me throbbing for her. I should have been angry, or at the very least annoyed, but I loved it. The tent I was pitching was proof enough of that.

"I'm serious," I said, moving in closer. "You are my weakness. I have never craved another's validation the way I do yours. That is why I need *you* to be the responsible one, too."

The confession felt heavier than I had intended, bringing a long silence. Instinctively, I nuzzled my face into the crook of her neck, seeking the safety I felt when close to her. My goddess, my anchor.

"Good boy." The words relaxed my tense body the moment they fell from her sweet lips.

There was still so much to be discussed, but this was a start.

Episode 21
Consequences

Cassie

Warmth. Pleasure. Unrestrained ecstasy.

My mind was lost in the fog of sleep, unable to understand the various sensations I was feeling. Scratching on my thighs, pleasure radiating from my core, faint moans of hunger, all familiar and just out of reach.

The slow descent from my hazy, dreamlike state shifted abruptly, causing a moment of panic. I was drowning in euphoria as my muscles tensed with an orgasm ripping me from sleep. By the time the waves of pleasure subsided, I was panting desperately for breath.

"What. The. Fuck," I gasp, still not completely coherent.

My head spun from the combination of a powerful orgasm and the disorientation that comes from waking from a deep sleep. I needed a moment to collect my bearings.

"Sunday morning worship," a deep voice replied from between my thighs, not realizing my exclamation was a statement not a question.

Professor Grant. The memories of last night washed over me as I became more aware of my surroundings. I was in my English professor's bed. My sexy professor.

His method of rousing me from sleep was more than a bit jarring for a multitude of reasons. As amazing as that orgasm was, Joshua's actions were a far cry from the *Mr. Boundaries and Rules* of last night. Hypocrite much?

A deliciously devious idea popped in my head.

"I hope that was worth the punishment," I said calmly.

My back arched as I reached for the ceiling, stretching my muscles. There is nothing in this world like a nice long stretch when you first wake up.

"Punishment?" Joshua questioned softly, shock painting his features.

I should have felt guilty watching the content smile dip into a worried frown, but I didn't. Instead, I felt an almost sadistic pleasure watching him struggle to figure out what he did wrong.

"I'm sorry. I just wanted to make you feel good," he said dejectedly.

Joshua's shoulders slumped in defeat as he gave me the saddest puppy dog eyes I had ever seen. It was almost too much to bear. Almost. Maybe if he hadn't made such a point to talk about roles and responsibilities last night, I would have let it slide, but here we were.

My face blanked, masking the high I still felt from an amazing early morning climax. Giving the professor a hard time would be difficult if he saw me smiling.

"I don't remember giving you permission to feast on me first thing in the morning, Joshua. Something like that needs to be earned.

Or you should have at least asked permission. Maybe we do need to elaborate on that little *boundaries* conversation of yours," I said sternly.

The color drained from his face as he listened, eyes widening in fear. The reaction would have been considered overdramatic if it had been anyone other than Joshua. Randomly spiraling into a quiet panic seemed to be his MO.

"I... I'm so sorry. I—Fuck!" he frantically rambled, leaping from the bed to put as much space between us as possible.

That's out of character. Every time we've been alone, Joshua has tried to be as close to me as possible. The new need for distance was more than a bit concerning.

Pacing around the room, Joshua raked his hands through his hair as he continued to mutter to himself. He reminded me of a trapped animal, terrified and ready to lash out if startled. This wasn't good.

"Joshua," I called softly, reaching out to offer a lifeline.

He looked down at my extended hand, then back at me with a pained expression that I didn't understand. If I could just get him to talk to me, then maybe I could talk him down.

"I didn't even consider consent. I'm so, so sorry. I never meant to... You have to believe me, Cassie." His voice strained as he choked back tears, trying so hard to keep from breaking.

The plea sent a chill down my spine and settled in the pit of my stomach like rotten food. This wasn't a meltdown over nothing like I thought. Joshua thought he crossed an enormous line and the torment of it twisted his features.

"That is why I need you to be the responsible one, too." The words from last night rang through my mind as their meaning finally became clear.

Actions have consequences, and I didn't bother to think about the implications of mine. I was only trying to tease the professor, play a little punishment game. *That he had no idea you were playing.* No, and how could he? We never got into the final details of things. *That's why he wanted to talk last night.*

I moved to the edge of the bed, settling myself as I tried to beckon the professor over again. God only knows what horrible things were running through his mind. *He thinks he violated the consent of a student so probably things like loss of job and jail.* That would make anyone freak out.

"Calm down, Joshua. You're not actually in trouble. I enjoyed the wake-up, I swear." I kept my voice calm and soothing, hoping it would disarm some of his fear.

He hesitated, the skepticism in his eyes unsurprising. My about face probably gave him emotional whiplash.

"But you said—"

"Miscommunication," I interrupted, hoping he would drop his guard enough to join me.

Some of the tension eased from Joshua's body as he slowly made his way to the bed. His steps were slow and shaky, like he was mere seconds from collapsing under the pressure he felt.

I kept an inviting expression plastered on my face, hoping to hide the total wreck I was inside. Joshua wasn't the only one feeling the pressure. One thing I've learned from our interactions is how much he takes his cues from me. It was a bit strange at first having an older man following my lead instead of the other way around, but the power of it had become a bit addictive until this mess.

"Knees, Professor," I quietly commanded when he reached the bedside.

With everything going on, I had expected some push back, but Joshua silently dropped to his knees and placed his head in my lap without any opposition.

"Good boy," I cooed as I ran my fingers through his hair.

Whatever tension the professor had held onto melted away as his body went limp. I watched the change in awe, admiring the beauty of his trust in me. Trust I took advantage of.

"I'm sorry. This got a little out of control. I only wanted to do a little fun punishment. I wasn't really mad." The apology hung between us, the silence deafening as I waited for his response.

I didn't push for him to acknowledge my words despite the anxiety that consumed me from his lack of response. *You deserve to squirm a little.* Unable to argue with the voice in my head, I quietly continued to pet Joshua, letting him take all the time he needed.

"I don't like punishments," he said, finally breaking the silence. His arms wrapped around my legs, holding me close as if he thought I might run away. "I like making you happy, not failing you."

That felt like a punch in the gut. This whole thing between us may be new, but the one thing I caught onto early was Joshua's eagerness to please. There was no way I could have guessed how over the top his reaction would be, but I shouldn't be surprised he reacted poorly.

"I think you were right last night. We need rules. Maybe we could have a conversation over breakfast?" I offered, silently hoping he wasn't going to just end things here and now.

I wouldn't blame Joshua in the least if he decided I was too immature to bother with after all of this. It wasn't as if he couldn't pull any woman he wanted. The man made panties melt. I wasn't so foolish to think he couldn't do way better than me.

Before I could get an answer, a loud pounding echoed through the apartment. Joshua nuzzled into my thighs and growled in annoyance when the booming sound wouldn't stop.

"At least he didn't use the damn key again," he mumbled as he rose to his feet.

Episode 22
Conversations in Cars

Cassie

I bounced uncomfortably, alternating my bodyweight from one foot to the other and back again. The sudden intrusion on our morning after everything that occurred left me anxious. My body itched with the need to assert myself in some way so I could regain my sense of control.

If it were just the two of us, I could easily recenter myself. A snap of my fingers, and Joshua would be back on his knees until we figured everything out.

Unfortunately, we were not alone. The presence of Joshua's friend Eddie added an extra layer to the tension that was already suffocating me. My suggestion the night before for him to bring us brunch had been made in haste. At the time, my only concern was getting the man out the door. I had given no thought to the fact that he would come back.

The frustrating part was that I seemed to be the only one still freaked out about this morning. If our misunderstanding from earlier was still stressing Joshua, he wasn't showing it. A casual smile tugged at his lips as he unloaded the bag of food while making casual conversation with the both of us. It wasn't fair that he could be the calm and collected host after completely falling apart less than an hour before.

"That reminds me," Eddie said as he presented me with another bag. "Stopped by and got you some cheap sweats so you don't have to parade around in Joshy-boy's shirt. Figured you weren't showing off your legs with me around because you wanted to."

"Oh, um… Thanks." I gave a timid smile as I accepted the offering.

Until that moment, I had forgotten how little I was wearing. The strange little eyebrow wiggle Eddie did in response had me break into a fit of giggles. A low growl of displeasure rumbled out of Joshua, an apparent warning to Eddie.

Arms in the air in surrender, he let out an indignant huff. "Dude, chill. I am definitely not moving in on your territory. I think we established last night that my plate is already full."

Clothes in hand, I moved toward the bedroom to change. As I passed Joshua, he pulled me into a passionate kiss that had my body melting into his. Instinctively, my fingers tightened and leveraged a firm grip. His surrender without hesitation cleared away the dark clouds from my morning.

Lost to the pleasure of the moment, I ground my hips into his body, pleasantly surprised to find him already hard for me. I craved his talented tongue and the sweet release it could bring me.

"Ah-hem." Eddie awkwardly reminded us that he was still in the room.

My cheeks burned with embarrassment as I realized Joshua's friend had a front-row seat to us dry humping. This was not my morning. Rushing out of the room, I left the two men to bicker in my absence.

The ride home, unlike brunch, was quiet. Without Joshua in the mix, Eddie and I had very little to discuss, it seemed. That was fine with me. I really didn't want to continue the conversation on why kissing one's best friend wasn't the five alarm emergency he thought it was. Do all men just stop maturing emotionally at fifteen?

"You two looked pretty cozy." Eddie's words broke through the silence. His face stayed neutral as his eyes remained on the road, giving me no hint as to what he was thinking.

"You don't sound thrilled," I remarked.

His lips curved into a smile, but he never removed his eyes from the road. "Thrilled my buddy is having what I hope is wild and crazy sex with a twenty-year-old? Of course I am."

Men.

"I'm twenty-one," I corrected him, earning me a chuckle. "Then what is your deal? Those looks while we ate weren't as subtle as you seem to think."

Silence fell over the car once more as the smile dropped from his face. It suddenly occurred to me that pushing the buttons of the forty-something-year-old man driving me home was not the best idea.

"The cozy part is what doesn't have me jumping for joy. You were supposed to be a rebound, not another possible disaster," he said with a sigh.

Did this man really just refer to me as another disaster? My fists clenched at the perceived attack. I get dumped on enough by grandmother dearest. There was no way I would let a stranger do the same, Joshua's friend or not.

Eddie glanced my way briefly and rolled his eyes. "Calm yourself. It has nothing to do with you."

"Really? Explain how I can be *another disaster* without it being about me," I demanded.

"Another *potential* disaster," Eddie clarified before muttering the word *women* with annoyance under his breath. If he hadn't been driving, I would have slapped the idiot.

"I'm surprised this Carla chick tolerated you long enough for you to assault her with your mouth," I shot back.

Instead of lobbing a comeback, Eddie shook his head and smirked.

"I'm not trying to pick a fight, kiddo. Chill out. I'm just concerned for my friend. You get that, right?" he said as if I was the one being an idiot. "It has zero to do with you as a person and everything to do with Joshua. How much did he tell you about Janet last night?"

The question caught me off guard, pulling some of the fight out of me. I didn't want to think about that name, not with so many questions still unanswered.

"Just that she's not a threat," I replied.

Eddie didn't say anything at first. The relaxed demeanor disappeared as tension filled his body. I couldn't help noticing the way his hands tightened around the steering wheel like he was trying to strangle it.

For some strange reason, I found joy in his reaction. I had no idea who Janet was, but I did feel threatened by her on some level.

Normally, people can't wait for an excuse to trash their ex, but not my professor. That knowledge had been festering in the tiny corner of my mind since last night. If I was being completely honest with myself, it was part of the reason I wanted to punish him this morning. I needed to know he wanted me enough to crawl a little and that he wouldn't just walk away.

"They were high school sweethearts. Broke up right before college, losing touch until our high school reunion," Eddie said, letting the statement hang in the air between us.

I'd be lying if I said I wasn't interested in hearing more about Joshua's ex, but it felt wrong coming from Eddie. I wanted to hear it from the man himself. This just made me feel gross.

I gave a shrug of indifference, hoping he'd get the hint, but Eddie continued. "I've seen him date, have one-night stands, be the ladies' man that commands the room... and I've seen him cozy."

The walls of the car felt like they were closing in. I didn't want to hear about Joshua with other women. I knew he'd likely been around the block and then some. The man was forty and hot. That didn't mean I wanted someone to paint a picture for me. Eddie needed to stop.

"Listen, it's sweet you care about your friend, but he is a grown-ass man—" I tried to throw some attitude his way, but Eddie cut me off, completely ignoring my interruption.

"And I've seen what happened when Janet snuffed the light right out of him."

That shut me up. Eddie paused for a moment and glanced my way. I nodded to signal he had my full attention now.

"Like I said before, it's not you. You seem sweet and all, but I need to know my friend is going to be okay. He shut down after Janet. And, no offense, but you *are* a student. That adds a whole new level to the mess. You can't be dumb enough not to see that. I need to know Joshua can come out of the other end okay this time."

If only Eddie knew. My status at PGU was significantly more complicated than just being a student. If our relationship came out, my grandmother would be out for blood. Guilt washed over me as I realized for the first time who truly had more to lose.

"Why did they break up?" My voice was barely a whisper.

"No idea. From what Joshua said, she dumped him over the phone with no explanation and then cut all contact," he replied.

My heart ached for my poor professor. So much was clicking into place. The constant need for reassurance and the fear of failure. Someone used to having the opposite sex throw themselves at their feet probably wasn't very versed in rejection. And to be dumped without being given any answers or closure... Janet didn't just break his heart. She broke his spirit.

The car slowed to a stop in front of my apartment. Unsure what else to do, I thanked Eddie for the ride and rushed inside.

Episode 23

Discombobulated

Joshua

Mondays, the most hated day of the week for many. Not for me. I spent most of the day buzzing with anticipation for my afternoon class, Cassie's class.

Living on the edge, I pulled out my phone to look at the picture she sent me this morning. There was no lingerie, just a closeup of her sweet cunt with two of her fingers pressing inside. Another morning of missed coffee, but worth it.

Despite the early morning indulgence, I was still overly eager to see my sweet goddess. The hunger I felt for her was a constant need that could not be satisfied. My cock throbbed as I locked my phone and placed it back in my pocket. I needed my head in the game before my afternoon class arrived.

I'd cut my lunch short so I could get the room prepared before students started to arrive. Ever since Cassie mentioned that Jonathan's advances were unwelcome, I'd been floating a few ideas around how to solve it. The winning solution was a bit juvenile, but it gave me the greatest satisfaction.

The class slowly started piling in, each noticing the names on the desks almost immediately. One by one, they quickly found their own names and sat in their newly assigned spots.

"I hope you all don't mind too much, but I thought assigned seats might help me learn names a little faster," I said with a chuckle.

There were a few whispers wondering why I didn't let them choose their own, but thankfully, no one challenged me. By assigning them myself, I was not only able to keep Jonathan away from my Cassie but also to make it so he couldn't even look at her during class.

Jonathan took his seat, his expression crestfallen as he looked around. Petty as it may be, I purposely surrounded him with students I hadn't noticed him speak to before. Cassie's seat was three over in the row behind Jonathan's so he couldn't look at her without it being obvious.

It took every ounce of my strength to not linger on Cassie when I glanced her way. The memory of how her body felt under mine kept worming its way into my mind, taunting me. I had to run the class sitting at my desk so I could hide the painfully hard erection that wouldn't go away.

The seconds ticked on, dragging out the sweet torture of having my goddess so close yet unable to do anything about it. Still, it was better than being apart.

Class ended without Jonathan looking toward Cassie once. Unless you count after class, but she was already halfway out the door. I couldn't help smiling at a job well done. *Maybe she will recognize my efforts and reward me.* That thought sent a thrill coursing through me.

Everyone else filed out of the room just as quickly. While it would be nice if Cassie could hang back and wait for the others to leave, I knew it was best that she didn't. My composure would dissolve in a matter of seconds and create problems for both of us.

The rattle of the door handle distracted me as I gathered my things. *Naughty little goddess already breaking what few rules we have.* The smile dropped from my face as a different student sauntered her way toward the desk.

"Do you have just a minute, *Professor Grant?*" Nausea overcame me as Valerie purred my name.

She was the last person I wanted to see. If I had known from the beginning that her brownnosing over the years was merely her testing the waters, I would have shut it down long ago.

"Actually, I don't. I have a meeting I can't be late to," I replied coolly, heading toward the door.

Being alone with the female students was always a recipe for disaster and doubly so when they had that heated look in their eyes. It was important to show complete indifference in situations like this. Any reaction was seen as an invitation.

Valerie stepped in my path with determination, blocking my escape. Her eyes fluttered as she tilted her head and gave me a warm smile. The hairs on the back of my neck rose as an unwelcome feeling settled over me. This was not her normal sucking up. This was different.

I schooled my expression, not wanting to expose my growing panic. Something like this happens every couple semesters. In the beginning, I was always so worried about overreacting. I never wanted to get a student in trouble because I misread their intentions. After the first year, I knew better.

The door was so close. I just needed to maneuver around the redheaded obstacle to reach freedom. I side stepped, letting out an exasperated huff as Valerie mirrored my movement. My sweaty palms shook with agitation as I tried to sidestep again and failed.

"This won't take long, Professor. I promise. If you would just give me a minute," she repeated her request.

My eyes dropped down, drawn to the movement as Valerie wrapped her arms around her body to hold herself. I realized too late she was slightly bent toward me and squishing her tits. It was a subtle move, one that could easily be played off as innocent, but the look in her eyes told a different story. She wanted me to look. *Dammit.*

"Please, *Professor*," she said, lightly caressing my arm. Her big, bright eyes looked up at me as she inched closer, pleading for me to play along.

I recoiled from her touch, lurching back to increase the distance between us. I needed more space. I needed to breathe. *Stay calm.* The beating of my heart roared in my ears, though I couldn't tell if it was in fear or anger. *Stay calm.* Nothing about this was right. I needed to leave.

"You know the procedure. Email me and we can schedule something," I said with cold detachment. There was no way I would meet with her alone after this, but Valerie didn't need to know that. Not yet.

"But Professor—" she began to whine before I cut it short. *Why do they think I will find whining attractive? It is so damn juvenile.*

"Email me, Valerie." The command boomed, causing her to flinch as I passed.

I hated being *that* guy. I hated that she forced me to be *that* guy. Why couldn't any of them ever leave me the fuck alone? If I wanted to have someone spread their legs for me, I'd ask. They didn't care. I was nothing more than a sexual achievement, or something they could brag to their friends about. The selfishness of it added to my frustration.

I let the door slam shut behind me without looking back. Normally, I would try to navigate a situation like that with more tact, but the boldness of her actions threw me off kilter. My hands were slightly shaking so driving was not an option. I needed somewhere I could be alone with my thoughts and calm down.

Changing direction, I headed to my office. No one would come looking for me there since Mondays weren't my normal office hours. It would give me the space to take a breath and recenter myself.

The trek to my office had never felt so long. I quickly entered, leaning my back against the door and drawing out a long sigh once inside. Safe. Quiet.

Walking to my desk, I slumped into my chair and stared at the ceiling. When did it become an uphill battle? It felt like interest from students was growing instead of waning each year.

The door to my office swung open, setting me on high alert.

"Jeez, Professor. You look like you're about to have a heart attack." *Cassie.*

I wanted to be relieved by her sudden appearance, but it only filled me with more apprehension.

"You shouldn't be here, Cassie. This isn't my office hours, and it will look suspicious," I tried to argue, but she ignored me by locking the door behind her.

"I was outside the room when you left. You looked pretty frazzled. I just wanted to make sure you were okay," she said with concern.

Her hips swayed with each step as she closed the distance between us. My heart raced with uncertainty. Was I excited or worried to be alone with her here? The last time Cassie was here, I lost control of the situation rather quickly. Then again, that was just the nature of our relationship.

"I'm fine," I lied, waving a hand dismissively.

Holding in a breath, I straightened my posture and waited to see if she would listen. This was a dangerous game to play here.

In true Cassie fashion, she ignored me and continued to saunter her way to my desk. My traitorous cock stiffened as she invaded my space and hopped on my desk in one graceful, fluid motion.

"Knees, Professor."

Every muscle in my body screamed in anger when I didn't immediately obey. I couldn't, not here. What if someone walked in? *She locked the door.* They could knock. *But they would have to know you are here. This isn't your normal hours. No one will come looking for you.* No, I have to draw a line somewhere. *But you don't want to.*

Ignoring the stupid voice in my head, I raised an eyebrow, ready to argue, but froze. Cassie's concerned expression had vanished and been replaced with one of authority as she pointed to the floor. My body moved without thought, dropping to my knees and nuzzling into her thigh.

"Such a good boy," she cooed softly as she ran her fingers through my hair.

The tension melted from my body as she caressed me like a favorite pet. I wanted to feel some sense of shame over what we were doing, but I couldn't find it in me. My mind was already floating away as I surrendered to my goddess.

"Do you want to talk about it?" The question made me pause. Up until this point, Cassie had been rather demanding of answers. This was new.

I debated unloading on her but stopped myself. She might feel jealous if she knew one of her classmates was being brazen in their attempts. It seemed cruel since there was nothing Cassie could do about it. Just one more thing in her life she couldn't control.

"Not right now," I whispered against her skin.

"Fair enough, but it seems like you could use a distraction," she said, spreading her legs.

A light giggle fell from her lips as I stared in disbelief. No panties. I shouldn't have been surprised, we've had this conversation before. Still, to know she had been sitting in class like this was more than I could process at the moment. Every class going forward was going to be spent wondering whether or not she was wearing anything under her clothing. I was never going to survive.

"Be a good boy and make me come, Professor."

Episode 24

Risky Behavior

Joshua

Only Cassie could make my entire world vanish by spreading her legs. All thoughts and worries melted away, and my mind focused on one thing—making my goddess come.

The softest moan fell from Cassie as my lips kissed their way up her thighs. My cock wept in response, begging for me to release it from my jeans and sink into her.

Wanting her so desperately and denying myself was a strange feeling. Being able to overcome my raging need to ravish her body and focus on her pleasure made me feel powerful, even if it was all based on her command.

Pain mixed with pleasure as Cassie's delicate fingers tangled through my hair, grasping a fistful. I loved how she took control by guiding my face to exactly where she wanted it, burrowed between her thighs. I didn't have to think or plan, only listen and obey.

My tongue sank into her cunt, and I almost came right there. *Fucking delicious*. A low groan rumbled through me as I began lapping up her dripping arousal, not a single drop wasted.

Before long, Cassie's legs trembled as her climax took hold. I continued to devour her through the waves of pleasure that had her thighs squeezing my head, not even pausing for air until her legs turned to jelly. A large, dopey grin overtook my face as I ran a hand over my beard soaked in her release.

Cassie steadied herself atop my desk, still panting for breath. She could barely hold herself up, drunk on the orgasm I gave her.

That's right. I am the one who made her come. Me. She looks properly fucked, and I only used my mouth. No one can please my goddess the way I can.

Still kneeling, I awaited her next command, secretly hoping it would be to taste her again. My mouth watered at the very thought.

Calm found Cassie as she reached out and ruffled my hair like a beloved pet. "Such a good boy."

The magic words. Never had anything sounded so sweet. *Besides her moans of ecstasy.* If I had a tail, it would have been wagging from the praise.

"Thank you, goddess."

The next few moments moved in slow motion. Cassie hopped off the desk, turning around to lean over with her skirt hiked up. Her perfect ass was eye level, tempting me to sink my teeth into her smooth, round skin. She was practically presenting herself, testing my limits.

"Now take your reward, *Professor*." I loved the way she called me that. It felt so wrong in all the right ways.

Like a fool, I stayed on my knees, frozen without more specific direction. Was I supposed to lick her again or fuck her? If it was based on what I wanted, either would be fine. I could always stroke myself while I buried my face back in her sweet pussy—

"Professor?" Cassie called out, breaking my train of thought.

"Yes?"

"Stand up and fuck me. *Now*." The authority in her voice sent a shiver through me. *Fuck*. That dirty little command had me ready to come in my pants.

I leapt to my feet, fumbling with the damn fly. My fingers shook with so much excitement that I couldn't get a proper grasp on the thing. Cassie snickered, watching me struggle as I cursed under my breath.

Way to go, Joshua.

After a few calming breaths, I steadied myself enough to free my cock from its denim confines.

Condom on, I gave myself a few leisurely strokes before lining myself up and slowly pushing in. Even after an orgasm, Cassie's cunt strangled my cock. The delicious squeeze had my balls aching to fill her.

Mine.

Overcome with the need to claim her, I grabbed Cassie by the hips. My fingers dug into her soft flesh, holding her so she couldn't escape.

Mine.

Tiny little moans fell from her lips, driving me to thrust harder, faster. I needed Cassie screaming my name. To my dismay, she buried her face in the desk, muffling her sweet sounds of pleasure. I doubled my efforts, determined to make her lose control.

Mine.

This was supposed to be my reward, and yet she withheld from me. In my frustration, I wrapped her hair around my fist and pulled until she arched toward me. Cassie would not be tamed. She clenched her mouth shut, refusing to give me more than her muzzled moans.

Mine.

It was both maddening and heavenly bliss. I loved that she challenged me, refusing to break. Nothing would ever be given freely, but only I was worthy enough to earn it.

"You. Are. Mine." I declared between heavy breaths. "Mine to worship. Mine to pleasure. Mine to fuck."

The mindless dribble continued to spill out of me while I fucked my whimpering goddess, driven by my need to possess her.

The pressure mounted until I couldn't hold back any longer. One final thrust and I exploded, my vision flashing white as the orgasm ripped through me.

Drained and dizzy, I stumbled backward until my legs bumped my chair.

"Careful there," Cassie teased as she eased me to my seat.

"That. Was. Phenomenal." I said between staggered breaths. I was still too high on the rush of dopamine to form better words.

"Not mad, then?" She asked while her hands tried to smooth the wrinkles from her skirt.

Mad? Why would I possibly be mad?

Cassie fought back a laugh when I didn't immediately answer. "For fucking on campus?"

Fuck.

I ran a hand down my face as I let it sink in. We had sex on campus, in my office. How stupid could I possibly be? At least I knew why she fought so hard to stay quiet. I on the other hand…

"I'm sure I will be once I come down," I confess.

"Good thing your office is out of the way, at least."

Cassie acted unbothered, but I could see the small crack in her façade. Her eyes kept glancing toward the door, as if she expected someone to knock at any moment. That would be a nightmare.

"We can't do this again, not here," I said with a frown.

If we were caught… I didn't even want to think about the trouble I would be in. Best-case scenario would lose my job. Fuck, this was stupid.

"No, no. I get it," she said, waving her hand to shush me. "That was pretty reckless. Won't happen again."

I wish I could believe her.

Cassie pulled out her phone, letting loose a frustrated huff.

"Shit. I need to get going, I have somewhere to be. Call me tonight?"

She didn't give me a chance to respond before giving me a peck on the cheek and rushing out the door.

"Of course," I mumbled to the empty room. She couldn't even wait long enough for me to get my dick back in my pants.

Alone, I began the daunting task of cleaning. Cassie had left in such a hurry that I didn't have the chance to tidy her up. She was running around campus post sex with no panties and a disheveled appearance. There was no way someone wouldn't realize she just had sex, and a sick part of me was thrilled by it.

Fuck. I'm going to lose my job and I don't even care, do I?

After wrapping the used condom in several loose napkins I kept in my drawer, I shoved it in my satchel. After all the other risks we took, there was no way I would chance the cleaners finding it while emptying my trash. I then scrubbed my beard with a few pumps of hand sanitizer. As much as I enjoyed smelling her on me, I couldn't walk around my job like that.

Satisfied that the more obvious traces of our indiscretion were taken care of, I sank back into my chair and stared at the ceiling.

That woman was going to be the end of me. I needed to be firm in setting boundaries, at least until she was responsible enough to be aware of our surroundings.

Just when I thought I was in the clear, a knock at my door draws my attention. The color drained from my face as a familiar feminine figure burst through the door, too impatient to wait for me to grant her entrance.

"Hello, Joshua. It's been a while."

Fuck.

Want more Obedience?

You don't have to wait for Volume Two! You can read episode 25 now on Kindle Vella* or by subscribing to my Patreon. More information at lizziebbrown.com

***Kindle Vella is currently available in the U.S. only.**

Stay in Touch

Want to know what Lizzie is up to before anyone else? Stay in the know by signing up for Lizzie's Naughty Little Newsletter. Visit lizziebbrown.com for more info.

Want to Read More by Lizzie?

Romance Serials

The Bucket List

A spicy, little picture and a summer apart. That's all it took for Carla and Eddie to go from BFFs to kinky bucket list buddies. Carla's long time crush was reignited, and Eddie was sent into a tailspin, wondering how their friendship would survive these new events. The Bucket List is a friends-to-lovers romance, following two friends who are about to become so much more.

Janet's Story

Months after a breakup, Janet felt like she was finally moving on. Then a phone call from a friend sent her back into a spiral of sadness and doubt. When things start to feel like they will never get better, a flat tire sets off a series of events that lead to not one, but two romantic possibilities. Which one will Janet pick? Who says a girl has to choose?

Note: Kindle Vella is available in the U.S. only. The Bucket List and Janet's Story can also be read by subscribing to https://www.patreon.com/LizzieBBrown.

Books

Friendsgiving with Benefits

Peanut butter and jelly, cookies and milk, macaroni and cheese. Some things were just better together, like Nixon and me.
We meshed well. It's why our arrangement lasted as long as it did. We were friends, roommates, and sometimes lovers. I mean, who better to help you during a dry spell than your adorkably sexy bff? But what happens when the lines start to blur between best friends with benefits and something more?

www.ingramcontent.com/pod-product-compliance
Lightning Source LLC
Chambersburg PA
CBHW071518110726
47908CB00003B/884